My Best Friend's Brother

Victoria Hall

Ordering Information

Special discounts are available on quantity purchases by corporations, schools, libraries, and others. For details, contact the author.

Library of Congress Cataloging- in-Publication has been applied for.

ISBN-13: ISBN: 978-1-7346503-9-6

ISBN-10: 1734650396

PRINTED IN THE UNITED STATES OF AMERICA.

Dedication

I first want to thank God for just giving me the courage on making this book happen. I want to thank my children: Frank Wise, John Harris, Tangela Harris, and Tracey Harris for the support and encouragement in writing this book. I want to thank my sister-in-Christ sister Lakeya Guy for editing my book, and for also encouraging me to pursue my dream. Last, I want to thank one of my coworkers Alonzo Goode for his support, his encouragement, and telling me not to give up. I will continue on writing books and pursuing my dream. Thank you everyone who will support me in buying my book.

TABLE OF CONTENTS

Chapter One 1

Chapter Two 29

Chapter Three 52

Chapter Four 58

Chapter Five 70

Chapter Six 80

Chapter Seven 89

Chapter Eight 102

Chapter Nine 113

Author's Bio 120

CHAPTER ONE

I t was a hot and sticky day, sitting here on my steps. My phone goes off. I answer and hear, "Hey girl, what's up?" It was Terri on the other end. I reply, "Nothing. About to head over to King of Prussia Mall to grab me an outfit to wear to the party at OD Park tonight." She responds with excitement, "Oh ok, I'm about to slide out with you then."

Terri is Lisa's best friend, after the girls grabbed them an outfit, they head back on the 99 bus to Norristown so they can get ready for the party. As they were walking up Green Street, they run into Terri's older brother Jimmy. "Hey Jimmy", says Lisa with a big smile on her face. Lisa was only 15 years old and Jimmy was 18. Lisa knew Jimmy was too old for her, but she had this big crush on him anyway. Jimmy asks, "Y 'all coming to the party at the park, tonight right?" "Yeah we will be there", said Lisa with a smile on her face. "Bet, I will see you there!", said Jimmy with a smile on his face.

Lisa was wearing a two-piece baby blue outfit. The shirt was strapless with a crisscross style in the back. The outfit was fitting really nice on her. She also had on a pair of baby blue three-inch heel shoes. "Girl there is a lot of people in this park, and the party is popping", Lisa looks around the park for Jimmy and spots him talking to some girl. "Terri who is that girl Jimmy is talking to?" Terri looks over where Jimmy is and asks Lisa "Why?"."Oh no reason I was just asking", Lisa replies. Terri says nonchalantly, "That is just Nook, some chick he be smashing from time to time, she's a nobody."

As Lisa sat back and watched Jimmy rub all over the girl, Terri says, "Come on let's walk around and see who is here'. While walking around Terri spotted her boyfriend Richard along with a few friends from around the neighborhood named Wayne and Kiara.

Jimmy walks up to them with a drink in his hand and asks, "Where are you all going?" Terri said, "Over here to talk to Richard". Terri and Richard have been seeing each other for about three months. Jimmy looks Lisa up and down and says nice outfit. Lisa smiles and says, "Thank you". Terri then walks over to Lisa laughing, "You like my brother, don't you?" "Girl we are best friends, I see how you smile every time he comes around". Terri shakes her head and laughs, "What's that all about?" asked Lisa to Terri. "Girl Jimmy is wild; he has got these females tripping over him and you are my girl, so I don't want you to get caught up in anything." It was now midnight and Lisa had to go home. She searches for Jimmy to tell him good night, but she couldn't find him. "Hey girl I'm about to head to the crib. I will check you out in the morning", says Lisa. Terri replies, "Ok girl I will see you tomorrow". Lisa walks off in disappointment, she knows that Jimmy left the party with that girl.

The next morning Lisa and her mother take a ride up to Chester to visit Lisa's dad. Lisa and her family were born and raised in Chester. Her mom and dad separated six months ago so her mom moved to Norristown to live with Lisa's grandmother's on Green Street. Terri lived the next block down from Lisa on Green Street and that's how they met each other and became best of friends ever since. Lisa has two older sisters, Linda and Laura, and an older brother Derris. Her siblings live in Chester with their father, but Lisa didn't want to live in Chester with him. She got into a lot of fights with the people in her school. Lisa and her mom head out to Chester. Lisa's dad owned his own construction company and several hotels in New York, Philadelphia, New Jersey, and planned to build one in King of Prussia.

Ms. Tanya and Nigel sat down to talk with Lisa. Her father explained to her that when she turns 21 years old that he wants her to be the manager of the new hotel that he is going to build in King of Prussia. He said, "I have some papers for you to sign. When you are old enough the deed to the hotel will be turned into your name". Lisa signs the papers and hands them back to her dad replying, "ok I will take them to my lawyer so he can finalize them".

"Mom, I'm going outside over to Dana's house, just call me when it's time to go", Lisa said. "So, have you been back to the doctor's yet?", asked Nigel. "No, I'm going back the end of the month and they will let me know what I will need to do from there" says Lisa's mother. Lisa's mother has cancer and she doesn't want to tell Lisa yet because she doesn't want to worry her daughter. She wants Lisa to finish school and not worry about anything but her schoolwork. "Nigel, I'm scared. I pray every day that I will live to see my baby graduate from high school. She has two more years to go and I don't want her to stress or worry about me", says Ms. Tanya. "I know, but you will have to tell her sooner or later because she's going to see that something is going on with you", says Nigel. "Ok, I will break the news to her later tonight on our way home." Ms. Tanya walks out on the porch and tells Lisa to go say goodbye to her dad.

Lisa and her mom get home and Lisa's phone rings. "Hey, what's up?" says Jimmy. Recognizing his voice Lisa replies, "Nothing just got back from seeing my dad, what's up with you and how did you get my phone number?" Laughing, Jimmy says, "Baby girl I have ways of getting what I need, enough of that do you want to take this ride with me to Philly? My family is having a block party. Sure, I guess, let me tell my mom I am going outside. "Lisa close and lock the door behind you", says her mom, "ok I will be back later" says Lisa.

Lisa gets in the car, "You look and smell good girl", smiles Jimmy. "Why thank you", said Lisa. Jimmy's phone rings. He answers, "Yo what's up? You on your way down here? Yeah why what's up? These boys ran down on Marcus again, pulled a burner out on him this time. Jimmy got quiet for a second, "ok bro I will be there in 15 mins".

"Is everything ok", asked Lisa, "yes everything is ok" he said in a stern voice. Lisa looks at him and turns her head to the window. She can see that Jimmy was upset about something but didn't want to ask him what was going on. They arrived at the block party and he introduces Lisa to his aunts and his cousins. He takes her over to where Mimi is sitting and says, "Lisa this is my number one cousin Mimi". "Hello" says Mimi, "hello" said Lisa. "Would you like something to eat or drink", asked Mimi. "No thank you not right now", Lisa replied. "Ok just let me know when you are ready to eat" says Mimi.

Marcus walks over and tells Jimmy he needs to talk to him. They walk off 10 minutes later; Jimmy comes back over to where the ladies are sitting and began talking with Lisa. Next thing you know an argument breaks out and then gunshots. Jimmy jumps up to run over to where Marcus is and sees his cousin lying on the ground with blood running from his body. Jimmy screams, "call 911, call 911". He holds his cousin's hand and tells him "help is on its way bro". Mimi starts crying, "That's my baby brother what happened? No!!!! Is he going to be alright?" Jimmy's aunt and cousin Kyle come running out of the house. Kyle says, "What happened I heard gunshots?" Jimmy's aunt Nae looks and sees that it was her son and starts screaming, "NO!!! What happened Jimmy? What happened?" and starts crying. An ambulance and the police pull up and they rush Marcus to the hospital. Lisa stands off to the side with her hand over her mouth in shock not knowing what to say. She hasn't seen stuff like this since her brother was shot in Chester when she was eight years old.

Jimmy grabs Lisa's hand and they run to the car to meet the ambulance at the hospital. Mimi and Kyle get in the car with them. Mimi is crying, Lisa rubs Mimi's back as they rush off to the hospital. They get to the hospital and Jimmy and Kyle step off. "Listen man I know it had to be them dudes from earlier, I just know it had to be them. Marcus beat the one boy up and that's why they came back with guns and shot him. Kyle they just started something that I'm going to finish says Jimmy", he looks Lisa's way and sees that she's looking at him. He turns back to Kyle and says, "Later we need to meet with everyone at the spot around 12 midnight". Nae and her older brother come running into the emergency room, Kyle walks over to his mother. "Kyle what happened to my baby? Will he be alright?" Kyle just looked at his mother not knowing what to say.

Two detectives walk over to Ms. Nae, "Hi my name is Detective Mars and this is Detective Brown". "Can you tell us what happened out there this afternoon?" asked Detective Mars. "Do you have any idea why someone would want to shoot your son?"

"Sir no I don't know why this happened, will he be alright? No one is telling us anything", says Ms. Nae. Kyle walks over and puts his arm around his mother and tells the detective, "please that's enough questions". The detective looks and says, "Ok we will be in touch with the family as soon as we find out some information about the case". "Kyle why is a detective talking to us, is Marcus going to be ok?". Mom he's going to make it, he's going to be alright, he will pull through this I promise you", as he hugs his mom.

Jimmy's phone rings and it is Raheem. "Bro what happened? I just got a call from Kayla". "Bro come down to Einstein Hospital." "Ok say no more, I'm on my way bro." Raheem is Jimmy's right hand man and best friend. They have been friends since the 3rd grade. Kyle said to Jimmy, "Listen I need to get mom to go home they are not going to tell us anything right now, so I need to take her home." "Yeah that would be best I don't want her to be stressed out", Jimmy said. "Bro be careful, Kyle said "You know me bro I will take a nigga out with no problem, NO problem!!!! I will be right back." Jimmy handed Kyle the keys. "Who is at the house with Kayla?" "Uncle Robert and I think one of Kayla's girlfriends. Raheem is on his way; we are going to get these niggas bro I mean that we are taking the whole family down. I just need things to die down before we make a move, so it won't look like we retaliated back on the family. We have to cover all grounds Kyle, all grounds", says Jimmy.

Kyle says to his mom, "Come on I'm taking you home, we will be here when the doctor comes out." "Kyle, I need to be here, I need to make sure that my baby is alright. Kyle, I need to make sure he is going to be alright", screams Ms. Nae. "Mom please let me take you home I will call you as soon as I hear something."

Kyle takes his mother by the hand and leads her to the car. "Kyle please make sure Marcus will be alright", cried Ms. Nae.

Kyle circled the block before pulling over and taking his mom into the house. Kayla ran over to her mom that was crying unconditionally. "Mom, Marcus is going to be alright. Do they know how many times he got shot?" asked Kayla. "I know I heard like five shots", says Kayla's girlfriend. "No, we're not sure exactly how many times but I believe one was in his chest area and it looks like one in his leg."

Back at the hospital, the ambulance brought in another shooting victim that was shot one time in the head. Jimmy looks at who it was, and it was the neighbor's son Jules, Mimi!!! "Look that's Jules, where was he at?" "I don't know Jimmy; remember we were over by the food." Jimmy calls Kyle, "Yo, they just brought Jules into the emergency room, he got shot in his head bro. Find out if anybody else got hit man."

"Yeah, I know his brothers are out here tripping man, Drop told me that when they were arguing and the boy shot Marcus, Jules then pulled on them and they shot him before he can get one off at them according to Drop. Drop said the same boys tried to rob Jules last week at the corner store."

"Jules' brothers are out here looking for them boys. Kyle fall back let them do what they have to, and we are going to sit on these niggas, we are going to watch their every move. They have a crib on 22nd and York right, yeah, well we will watch that house, we will follow them if we have to switch cars up as we follow them. Kyle listen we are going to get these niggas I promise you that. I do not care if we have to sit on that house for weeks at a time, we will get them."

Jimmy looks and he sees that more police started coming into the emergency room asking questions to the family.

Kyle finally came back and Jimmy said to his cousins that he has to leave and take Lisa back home. "I will call you once I get back to Norristown." Jimmy gives Mimi a hug and Kyle a pound then slides out the side door. In the car it was silent all the way home, Lisa knew that Jimmy was upset.

They arrived in Norristown, Jimmy's phone rings and he looked at the number and said this chick here. "Hello", answered Jimmy "I need you to come over I'm going in labor", "Listen I don't have the time to come over there I'm busy", and Jimmy hung the phone up. "No, this nigga didn't hang up on me", says Nook. She calls back but it was no answer. Jimmy phones rings again and its Nook again, "Yo please stop calling me I'm not taking you to the hospital nor am I coming up to the hospital. Please stop calling my phone", says Jimmy and hangs up the phone. Lisa's phone rings and it's her mother, "Hello mom is everything ok?" "Yes, I just need to talk to you", says her mom. "Ok I will be there."

"Is everything alright?", asked Jimmy. "I don't know my mom sounded funny on the phone, like she had to tell me something", said Lisa. "Ok I will drop you off", says Jimmy.

Lisa walks into the house and her mom is sitting in the chair crying. "Mom what's wrong? Is everything ok?" "No Lisa sit down I have something to tell you." Lisa sits on the side of her mom and holds her hand. "Lisa I been trying to hold back from telling you this because I don't want you to worry." "What is it mom tell me?", says Lisa with tears in her eyes not knowing what her mom has to tell her. "Lisa, I have cancer and it's stage two, I don't know if they can do anything about it." "No mom" cries Lisa, "when did you find out that you have cancer?" "I knew for some time. I didn't want you to be in school worrying about me and can't get your schoolwork done." Lisa lays her head on her mother's lap crying, "baby everything is going to be alright I promise you. I been taking chemo to see if they can get rid of the cancer so please, I don't want you to worry, ok sweetie." Lisa nods her head yes, "Baby I want to go lay down help me up the steps". Lisa helps her mother up to her room. "Do you need anything?" Her mom replies, "No baby I'm ok for right now." Lisa sits on the couch crying; she tries calling Jimmy, but his phone went right to voice mail. "Jimmy where are you I really need you right now? I need someone to talk to please call me back once you get this message."

With all that is going on Lisa just wanted to be with Jimmy by his side. She needed to be in his arms right now. Lisa calls Jimmy's phone again, and again it went to voice mail. Lisa's mind starts racing all over the place. Is he with Nook at the hospital or is he back down at the hospital with his family?

Jimmy meets back up with Kyle at the hospital. Mimi walks over to Kyle and hands him the phone, Kyle looks and says, "who is this?", it's Raymond. Raymond is Mimi's boyfriend and also a hitman for a lot of people in the city. But Kyle is also a man that can do a lot of harm to people too. "Yo bro what's up? You need me just say so I'm there. I'm sitting right in front of these niggas house right now." "Nah bro come down to the hospital so we can talk." "Say less be there in 10", Kyle hands the phone back to his sister. As they all sit and wait to hear something from the doctors Raymond comes in the hospital with a killer look on his face. Mimi goes over to him and hugs him crying, Raymond hugs his girlfriend back. He sits Mimi down and says, "I will be right back let me talk to your brother and cousin for a minute."

Jules mother and younger brother comes running into the emergency room. "Hi, I'm looking for my son he was brought here they said he was shot." Kyle walks over to Miss Reed, Miss Reed turns and looks, "Kyle what is going on, what happened here?" "Miss Reed Marcus and Jules was robbed by some boys over on 22nd Street. Marcus saw one of the boys and they got into a fight. I guess Jules was there and the boys came back while the block party was going on and shot Marcus. I'm not sure where Jules was at when he got shot. We saw the ambulance bring him in and that's all we know. We don't know if he was outside at the block party no one knows where or how he got shot." Miss Reed falls into Kyle's arms crying, "They said he got shot in the head Kyle, not my baby please tell me something." Miss Reed turns back to the nurse sitting at the desk. The nurse says, "Miss it's not much we can tell you right now, but both of the men are in surgery and the doctors will be out to talk with both families as soon as they can."

One of the doctors came out and asked, "Who's the family for Jules Reed?" "I am" said Miss Reed "I am his mother."

"Can we talk over here please? I'm sorry we tried everything we could to help your son, but he didn't make it?"

"NOOOO!!!", shouted Miss Reed as she fell to the ground. Her son ran over to his mother and asked, "What did the doctor say mom what did he say?" "Jules didn't make it! Jules didn't make it", as she cried hugging her son. Bruce grabbed his mom as she was falling to the ground crying, "Why!!!! Why?" Detective Mars and Brown walked over to Miss Reed and

Bruce. "We are sorry for your loss, but we need to ask you some questions regarding the shooting of your son." Bruce snapped, "What you mean you need to ask some questions!!!! My mom just lost her son and I lost a brother, we not answering no questions." Kyle came over and put his arm around Bruce, "Come on man you have to calm down". "Kyle my brother is dead man he's dead and you think my moms can answer these dudes' questions?" Kyle walks over to the detectives, "Do you all think you can do this another time, come on they just lost a son and brother. Miss Reed doesn't know nothing she wasn't even home when all this happened."

The two detectives said ok and walked off. Jimmy kept watch at the detectives and the police that was in the hospital. It was so many family and friends there. Police and detectives were questioning any and every one that was at the block party.

Lisa calls Jimmy's phone again, "Jimmy please call me back, I need to talk to you, it's about my mom so please call me back. I hope you're alright please call me back once you get this message please."

Meanwhile back at the hospital another doctor comes and calls out, "Who is the family for Marcus Smith?". Jimmy, Kyle and Mimi stood up, "We are his family, how is he doc?", said Jimmy. "We performed surgery on Mr. Smith, he lost a lot of blood. The surgery went well and he's going to go to the ICU once he comes out of recovery." "Thank you, doc, when can we see him?" "He's not out of the woods yet, he is still in critical condition and still fighting for his life." Mimi starts crying, "You just said that the surgery went well but he's still in there fighting for his life, How?" "Mr. Smith was shot four times, one of the bullets was close to his heart, we're unable to reach that bullet and we're afraid if we try that we might lose him. Also, he lost a lot of blood, so we are giving him a blood transfusion as we speak. We will keep the family updated with any changes." "Thank you, doctor", said Kyle.

Kyle's phone rings and he answers, "Hello." "Yo bro, where's Jimmy? I been calling his phone and no answer." "He is here with us hold on." Kyle passes the phone to Jimmy. "Bro where is your phone at?" Jimmy looks in his pockets, "It has to be in the car bro, what's up?" "Meet me outside I'm about to pull up." "Kyle come on; Raheem is outside." Jimmy gets his phone out of the car and sees that Lisa has called him six times and left messages. Raheem told Jimmy and Kyle that he sat at the house on 22nd and York. "Bro these dudes think it's sweet, they are sitting out there chilling and drinking like nothing happened." Raheem started pacing back and forth. "I wanted to take them out right then and there but bro you didn't answer the phone." "Rah man we going to get them we just need to let it die down, all them police in there they seen all of our faces. Bro Jules didn't make it, so you know his brothers are going to be out there looking for them too. I just don't want anything to come back on us, that's why I'm saying fall back."

"Raheem, Jimmy is right" says Raymond that was already outside smoking a cigarette. "If you all go after them right now the cops will come to your doorstep first." Raymond says. "Raheem they will be caught slipping trust man you already see what they are doing right now. They are sitting back getting high not paying attention. We just watch them and once this dies down a little then we come for them." "Alright bro you are right. I just wanted to take them niggas out like my blood was boiling cause they out there celebrating bro." Jimmy walks away and calls Lisa back, "Hey baby girl what's the matter?" asked Jimmy once Lisa answered the phone. Lisa starts crying "Jimmy, where are you?" "I'm at the hospital" Lisa gets quiet. "Hello", "Yeah I'm here" says Lisa. "You up there seeing the baby?"

"Lisa I'm not worried about Nook and that baby. I told you I need to make sure that the baby is mines before I go and play dad. I'm not going up there and sign no papers or even act like I'm the dad until the blood test comes back. Now what's up with you?" "Jimmy I just found out that my mom has stage two cancer", cries Lisa. "Jimmy, I need you to tell me that everything will be alright." "Lisa baby girl I'm sure that everything will be ok, you just have to be there for your mom as she deals with this baby. You just have to make sure that she gets all the care that she needs, I am here for you if you need anything. I will pay for her medicine if you need me, I will go with you to all her appointments. Lisa I am here for you. It's late and I want to come and see you before you go to bed but we're still down here at the hospital, Marcus is out of surgery but he's not out of the woods yet. He still has a bullet left in his chest; they didn't want to remove it cause it's too close to his heart. Also, the other man that was shot, Jules, he didn't make it. Lisa there is a lot that is going on right now. I know you need me, and I'm going to try and make it up there tonight. If it's too late baby girl, I will see you in the morning I promise you". Ok says Lisa, "Jimmy please be careful out there."

"Baby girl I will, and I will call you later on tonight to tell you good night ok?" Lisa agrees, "Yes talk to you later." It's now 7am and the guys are sitting in the car watching the house on 22nd and York in North Philadelphia. They see Jules little brother drive past them in a black car with tinted windows and no license plate on the car. "Hey, isn't that Jules car right there driving past slowly?" asked Kyle. "Yeah it is his car and that's his little brother driving it. What is this little nigga up too, he going to get himself hurt or locked up?" The car speeds off and another car pulls up slow and you hear POP POP POP POP AND screeching of tires going down the street. Jimmy didn't move his car; he was so far back in the cut no one knew he was even sitting there.

"Look these niggas peeking out the window, yeah I think little nigga messed this up for us cause now these dudes are going to be on watch now. I think we really need to fall back and wait this out" said Jimmy. Raheem makes a phone call to New York. "Yo Jimmy we don't even have to take care of this problem Brick said he got it just send him the location and he got from there."   Jimmy didn't say nothing he just sat there looking at the house trying to figure out what these niggas was going to do next after their house was just shot up. You can hear sirens and the police came from all different directions. They knock on the door and there wasn't any answer. "There's no answer at the house", said one officer on his walkie-talkie. They walk around the back of the house and see no movement.

"Yo I think these niggas ran out the back door, wait look they entering the house", said Jimmy. "No one is in the house", says the officer. The guys sit there to see if there is anyone in the house no one was in there.

As Jimmy pulled off nice and slowly he stared at the house trying to figure these niggas out. Jimmy was one that will study you and will figure you out in no time. As Jimmy was dropping everyone off his phone was ringing. "Hey baby girl, I'm sorry. I will be in Norristown in a half." Lisa said, "Ok see you when you get here. Jimmy I'm scared, my mom been up in her room all morning and hasn't come down for anything to eat." "Did you go check on her?" asked Jimmy. "Yes, she said that she wasn't hungry. I called my dad and he's on his way here now", cried Lisa. "Baby girl I'm almost there I will see you soon", said Jimmy. Lisa says, "ok" and they hang up.

14

"Mom", Lisa calls upstairs, "do you need anything?" Lisa walks up the steps because she didn't hear an answer from her mom. "Mom you ok?" "Yes baby. I'm fine. I was just in the bathroom taking a shower." Lisa starts crying looking at her mother's frail body as she walks out of the bathroom. Here, let me help you to the bed. "No baby, I want to sit in the chair and watch TV." Lisa sits her mother down in the chair and turns the TV on. A knock at the door startles Lisa. "You ok?" "Yes baby. Go get the door." "Ok it's probably dad I called him." "Who's there?" asked Lisa. "It's me baby girl, your father." Lisa opens the door and gives her dad a big hug. "Daddy, mom doesn't look right. She makes it seems like she is ok when I know that she's not." "Baby she will be ok. She just needs plenty of rest." Nigel walks upstairs into Ms. Tanya room. "Hey, young lady. What's going on with you?" asked Lisa's father. "Hey Nigel, I could be better. Most days are good other days are bad, and today isn't a good day. I just need some rest and I will get through this day. The chemo some days has me feeling tired. Nigel I'm trying to hold on for my baby girl, I don't want to leave her, she needs me." "Tanya let's just take this day by day ok?" "Yes, you're right I will take it day by day."

Another knock at the door and it was Jimmy. Lisa gives him a hug crying, "baby girl it's going to be alright I'm here now." "Jimmy, my mom is so sick, and I know that she is trying to hold on for me to finish high school. I know she doesn't want to leave me. Jimmy, I don't want to lose my mother either." "No matter what happens Lisa I will be here for you." Jimmy took Lisa by her face and said, "I will never leave your side no matter what." Lisa didn't know what to say. She really liked Jimmy, and in her heart, she knew that he liked her too, but she also knew that he has a newborn baby that she could never compete with.

Lisa's father comes downstairs. "Hello sir" Jimmy says. Nigel reaches his hand out to shake Jimmy's hand. "Dad this is Jimmy, Jimmy this is my dad." "Is this your friend, Lisa?" asked her father. "Yes, daddy we're just friends, it's not what you think".

"Ok I trust you, and Jimmy I am going to put my trust into you too. I know my daughter needs a friend right now, cause of all that she is going through with her mother being sick. My daughter knows how I feel about her with a male friend at a very young age. Young man may I ask how old you are?" "Sir I'm 18 years old", Nigel looked at Lisa. "My daughter talks about you a lot Jimmy I know that she needs you here to help her out. I will leave you with this, Jimmy my daughter is only 15, I know that she will be 16 in three weeks, but my daughter seems to like you a lot."

"I know that he's more than just a friend, cause Lisa you could have called a female friend instead of Jimmy, so I know that she likes you. I just want my daughter to finish school. I really want her to go off to college but with her mother being sick I don't think that is going to happen. I don't want my daughter pregnant at a very young age." "Sir your daughter and I have never had sex and I respect that she's 15 years old. I respect your daughter I will never hurt her or leave her side. Sir you don't have to worry about a thing I will make sure that Lisa and her mother is well taken care of."

"Do you have a job? Are you still in school?" asked Nigel. "Yes, sir I do have a job and I graduated from high school this year in May", says Jimmy. "Lisa, I like your friend, he's well respectful, nice and neat looking. So, you two just hang out with each other?" asked Nigel. "Yes sir", says Jimmy. "Sir I respect that she's younger than me, but I really like your daughter and I enjoy her company." "Listen I just want the best for my baby girl. This here is new to me. I have known my daughter to fight boys not being in a relationship with one. Now I will put my trust into the both of you, and Jimmy I hope I don't have to come back down here for anything but to see my baby girl and her mother." "Sir, I promise you I will wait to be in a relationship with your daughter."

"What type of work do you know how to do?" asked Nigel. "Well I know how to do a lot sir, I use to help my father build houses from the ground up when I was 16 years old. He passed away last year." "Oh ok", said Nigel, "I might have some work for you in a couple of months. I will let my daughter know when the job will be ready, and you can contact me with all your information." "Ok sir thank you."

"Lisa call me if you need me, make sure you keep an eye on your mother." "Ok daddy I will." "You know what I told you. I'm putting my trust into the both of you. I don't need my daughter getting pregnant at a very young age." "Sir I promise. It's not like that we're just friends". See ya"ll later. Lisa don't forget to keep checking on your mother." "Ok Dad I will."

"I kinda like your dad, he seems like a real down to earth guy." "Jimmy my dad owns a lot of hotels and he can get you into his business. A lot of people respect him in Chester. The police and all the important people really respect him.

"I feel that he likes you too because you being 18 years old and me 15. Man I really thought he was going to be tripping." Jimmy phones beeps. He looks and his face expression made Lisa ask "is everything alright Jimmy?" "Yeah it's Nook she wants me to come to the hospital and see the baby." "Jimmy why don't you just go, she's not going to stop calling or texting you unless you come there and see the baby. I'm ok and if I need you I will give you a call, keep your phone on you this time around Jimmy."

Jimmy kissed Lisa on her forehead, "I will see you later, after I come from the hospital with Nook I will be going down to see my cousin and my family. I will call you later", "ok" said Lisa.

Jimmy gets to the hospital and sits in the car for a second. He has Lisa on his mind and can't shake it off. Jimmy fell in love with Lisa but doesn't have the desire to let her know yet. He knows that he will have to wait to be intimate with her. But he just wants to hold her in his arms all night and wake up beside her.

Jimmy finally gets out the car goes into the hospital to maternity where Nook and the baby are. Knock, knock. Jimmy enters the room, "It's about time you came to see your daughter", said Nook. "A lot happened in the last two days Nook and I didn't have the time to get up here." "What that little girl you be talking to stopping you from seeing your child." "She has nothing to do with me not coming up here. I need to take a blood test to make sure that this child is my child." Nook starts laughing, "When I see your little girlfriend, I'm going to let her know what time it is. She is not going to keep my daughter's dad away from her Jimmy and I mean that."

Jimmy picks the baby up and stares at her, "What's her name asked Jimmy?" "I named her after me, Narlyn." "Why she so light?" "Jimmy all babies come out light skin." "I don't see any dark spots on her fingertips. Nook, I'm not saying that she's not mines but I need to get a blood test as soon as possible." "Ok whatever Jimmy we can do that soon as we leave the hospital. You only asking for a blood test cause of that little girl you mess with." "She has nothing to do with this. You don't even know her and you have a problem with her." "My problem is that she trying to stop you from seeing your daughter Jimmy." "Nook my little cousin got shot the other night Jimmy yelled. I was down at the hospital with my family. Plus, you are not my girl that I have to answer you when you call. I'm going through enough right now dealing with this. I didn't come up here to hear you talk bad about Lisa, someone who doesn't even know you."

Jimmy puts little Narlyn down and grabs his keys and walks out the door. Nook started crying, "When I see this little girl, I'm telling you Mya I going to smack the mess out of her."

"Nook you can't get mad at her because he didn't come and see Narlyn. He said his little cousin got shot and he was at the hospital." "Mya he still could have answered my calls. I talked to him that day and told him I needed a ride to the hospital that I was in labor and he hung up on me. I am going to take her and get a blood test to shut him up and make that little girl look stupid. I know it's his baby. She can be red, yellow or blue I know she is his." Mya laughs, "Nook I just think you are wrong about the chick."

"Hello, Hey Jimmy, Mom wants to see you", says Terri. "Ok I am about to pull up now. Yo Terri I go to the hospital to see the baby and this chick is like why that little girl you are messing with stopping you from seeing your baby. Sis I don't even know if that's my baby." "Yeah right cause I know for a fact that she was still messing with Bill" says Terri. "But what's up with you and Lisa?" "Sis I really like shorty and I know she's underage but I'm really feeling her. I met her dad today Terri." "Oh, really and what did he say about y'all age difference?" "Not much really. All he said was that he wants Lisa to finish school and don't want her to get pregnant at a young age. I can respect that sis. I really don't have any plans on sleeping with her right now."

"Her 16th birthday is coming up and I want to give her a surprise birthday party in the park." "Oh ok big bro" Terri says laughing, "you really do like her." "You might not see this picture right now but mark my words I'm going to make her my wife." Terri starts laughing, "ok Jimmy just come see what mom wants" as she is still laughing while she hangs the phone up.

Jimmy walks in the house and Terri just shakes her head, "what?" asks Jimmy. "I'm serious about this, she's going to be my wife" Jimmy says as he walks up the steps to his mother's room. "Hey mom what's up?" "Jimmy you been back down to the hospital to see Marcus?" "Mom I just left there this morning." "My sister just called and said someone came to the hospital to see Marcus but when the detective asked him for ID the man got aggressive and walked out of the hospital. The officer went behind him and the gentleman ran and jumped into a car that had no license plate on it. She said the car was black with tinted windows." "Wait we left the hospital around 2am. Mimi was still there?" "Yes, Mimi was the one that called the detective and said that the man wasn't related to her family and that she didn't know who he was. My sister is worried that they might come back and do something to Marcus." "Ok mom I will take care of it, I'm going back to the hospital now."

Jimmy pulls up to the hospital and Mimi is still there with Kyle, Kayla and his aunt. "Oh my god Jimmy I am so scared right now. I want them to move my son to another hospital, but they are telling me that they can't because of his condition." "Yes, they said with the bullet still in Marcus chest it can cause damage if they move him."

Jimmy and his aunt were talking. Two detectives walked up and started asking questions. Jimmy's aunt told the detectives that whoever shot

Marcus was coming back to finish the job. I want protection around my son 24 hours. "You hear me?" said Jimmy's aunt Nae.

"Hello", says Jimmy as he answers his phone. "The job is done. I will hit you back" and Raheem hangs up. Jimmy pulls Kyle to the side and tells him that Raheem got one of the boys that shot Marcus. They give each a pound and walks back over to the detective. "Sir my aunt is right, if they tried to go into my cousin's room one time they will try again and this time we might not be here to see who it is. We will leave names of who can come and visit. They will need to stop at the nurse's station before they can enter into his room. I don't care if something goes down in this hospital there will be a cop by his room door at all times" said Jimmy.

Jimmy and Kyle meet up with Raheem, Raheem tells them what happened and how he took one of the guys out that shot Marcus. "Listen these dudes are slow" says Raheem. "I sat on that house all night and watched these guys party and when they were caught slipping and I made my move. I got rid of everything, the car, the gun and walked three blocks over and took an Uber from there to the hospital." "Good move" said Jimmy, "we want no trace back to anyone of us."

Uncle Robert walked in the hospital, he walked to the men and said 'there was another murder late last night, one of the men on York Street got killed on the corner of their house. The Police is at Jules's mom house questioning the brothers about the murder last night." "So, they don't have any witnesses" asked Jimmy. "I don't think so, but there's more, right after what happened last night no more than 10 mins after the killing a car came down the block and started shooting but I guess really wasn't aiming for anyone. Whoever it was they were stupid to start shooting while the cops were still out there. The cops caught the person shooting the gun out the window of the car at the end of the block."

Kyle looked at Jimmy, "So these dudes think that Jules's family wasn't going to do anything? Their brother just got killed." "Listen I'm just telling y'all to stay low until this blows off" said their uncle Robert.

"What do we have to stay low for? We had nothing to do with it" says Kyle. "I know y'all didn't but after the detectives finish questioning Jules's family trust me they're coming to this family next. And the fact that someone tried to come in this hospital and into Marcus's room they have all the right to come question this family."

"Hello" answers Jimmy. "Hey, is everything ok with you?" asked Lisa. "Yeah, we just down here at the hospital, somebody tried to go into Marcus's room while Mimi was here and she never seen the guy before. My mom called me when I was leaving your house and told me to go down to the hospital that my aunt Nae needed me." "Oh wow, is he ok they didn't try anything did they?" "No Mimi called the detective that was in the hospital and told him that there was someone going into her brother's room and he wasn't family." "They locked him up right?" "No, he left before the detective got there. Now my aunt is all upset and wants us to take turns being down here with him."

"Lisa I will call you right back there are some detectives coming to talk with the family." "Ok please call me back." "Hi, my name is Detective Robinson, and this is Detective Nelson. We are investigating the shooting of Daryl Ryan. He was murdered last night. Did you hear anything about the killing?" No, all we know is that someone came here and tried to get into my son's room to hurt or even kill him and you coming here asking us questions about someone getting killed last night?" says Ms. Nae. "Y'all got some nerve, why you not out there trying to solve the shooting of my son?"

"Uncle Robert, can you take mom into the room with Marcus so we can talk with the detectives?" "I'm sorry about what my aunt said sir but she's right. My little cousin was shot two days ago, and no one came to see our family after the day it happened." says Jimmy. "Then this man comes into the hospital and tries to go into his room. If his sister wasn't here this would be another murder that you're going to have to solve.

"So, you're telling me that neither one of y'all had anything to do with Daryl Ryan's murder or the drive by shooting of the house he was living at two nights ago?" "Sir as we said we know nothing about what is going on." "So, you have an alibi to where you were at last night?" asked detective Robinson. "I was with my girlfriend and her father talking about a job", says Jimmy.

"And sir can you tell us where you were last night?" "I was at home with my mother making sure our house was safe", said Kyle. "I don't live down here" says Raheem, "I was called yesterday to come to the hospital cause a family member was shot." "Ok here's my card if you hear anything please feel free to give us a call." Jimmy started laughing as he snatched the card out of the detective's hand. "We not no snitches, so please try to go find the person who did this to my little cousin."

"Robinson, we have to go, there was another shooting said the detective." "Man, I told you I got this, every last one of them niggas are done" said Raheem "and that's all you need to know, I got this." Now Kyle knew Raheem for years, but he doesn't know him like Jimmy knows him. Jimmy started laughing and shaking his head. "Man, this is why I love you like a brother because you are my brother" as he hugged Raheem. Jimmy says to Kyle, "Little cousin you wouldn't understand" as he laughed again and walked away.

Uncle Robert walked over to Kyle and said, "I'm going to take your mother home so she can get some rest. Mimi said she needs to go too so she can get a change of clothes." "Mimi you need to get some rest too", said Kyle. "I'm not leaving my baby brother here by himself after what just happened today. We need to take turns staying here", said Mimi. "Mimi is right" said Jimmy. "Whenever these dudes think they can come up here and do something to Marcus they will. That means someone will need to be here at all times. Mimi we'll stay here until you come back", says Jimmy. "Just get some rest we are not going anywhere."

"Hello", Jimmy answers his phone. "Jimmy we're leaving the hospital today", says Nook. "I apologize for how I was acting earlier; I should have taken what you said about your cousin into consideration and not blame your little girlfriend." "Here you go again about Lisa, I told you she is the one that told me to come see the baby. I wasn't coming up there until I took a blood test. I told you if the baby is mines Nook, I have no problem in taking care of my child." "I will give you a blood test if that's what you want Jimmy, that's not a problem because I know for sure that you are Narlyn's father." "Nook what's up what did you call for?" "I was just telling you that we were leaving the hospital today and if you want to come see the baby tonight you can." Jimmy laughs a little, "Nook I won't be able to see her tonight, I'm down in Philly at the hospital with my family and it will be too late for me to come see her when I get back to town."

"Jimmy you can come see her anytime of the day or night. You can spend the night with her if you like." "Look Nook I will try to see her when I can right now will not be a good time ok." "Ok but I bet you will be on Green Street at that little girl's house tonight." "I don't got time for this Nook and if I want to go see her tonight I will that's none of your business", and Jimmy hung the phone up.

"Kyle we will take turns staying here with Mimi. Well tonight her and Raymond will be here and knowing Mimi she will be here every night." So, they all sat down and Jimmy tells them how he really likes Lisa. "Lisa, how come I never met this chick?" said Raheem laughing. "Why you are hiding her from your brother?" "Raheem you will meet her real soon, she's the one I'm going to marry." Kyle turns to his cousin, "You are talking about the girl that was at the block party?"

"Yes" says Jimmy. "She looks very young man." "She is young and I'm going to be with her til' death do us part man, I really love this girl."

Raheem starts laughing, "What you fell in love with the sex?" "No man I haven't had sex with her yet, I haven't even kissed her in her lips yet." Raheem and Kyle look at Jimmy with a surprised look on their faces. "Ok wait so you mean to tell me that you're in love with a chick that you have not had sex with or even kissed her in the lips?" said Raheem. "Yes, man it's not like that, she's worth the wait, plus she's only 15 years old." "Jimmy, man are you trying to go to jail for this girl or what?" "Raheem bro it's not like that, we hangout we laugh she makes me happy. Even on my worst days she seems to bring a smile on my face. Plus, she will be 16 in three more weeks." "So that makes it legal when she turns 16?" asked Raheem. "No man I told you I'm going to wait until she turns 18 before, I do anything with her. Plus, I made her dad a promise that all we are is friends. I'm just going to let you meet her and you will see that she's the one for me. Her dad said that he will let me work with him doing construction."

"So, you met her dad already?" Raheem said. "Raheem I'm telling you this girl is about to change my life around."

Mimi and Raymond walk into the hospital. "We are going to talk about this later" said Raheem. "Hey what's up Raymond?" "Bro I thank you for staying here with my sister" said Kyle. "Call my phone if y'all need anything, if any changes, happens or if something doesn't look right." "No worries" said Raymond as he lifted up his shirt and showed his piece. "Ok I will catch up to y'all later" says Jimmy. "Where are you going to see your young tender roni?" says Raheem laughing. "Yes, I'm going to see my wife" said Jimmy with a smile on his face. Mimi turns and looks at her cousin, "You are talking about the girl that was at the block party?" "Yup" said Jimmy smiling. "Yeah he says he thinks he is falling for this 15-year-old girl that he's about to go to jail for." "Man, I told you it's not like that, she's still a virgin" laughs Jimmy. "Right now, I just like hanging out with her, talking, laughing and just having fun that's all."

"I'm giving her a surprise birthday party in two weeks at the park in Norristown." "A birthday party" said Raheem, "man what this girl got over you?" "Nothing I just really like her, and I want to spend the rest of my life with her. Listen y'all may think I'm tripping right now but I really like her." "Ok, you my brother and if you like her, I like her" says Raheem. "She seems like a nice girl" said Mimi. "She seems like she's smart, intelligent, and a little shy too when you first meet her. I really didn't meet her face to face but I can say that she was here for Jimmy when my brother got shot, she made sure Mimi was alright, got drinks for the family and everything."

"Well I'm about to head back to town I will get up on y'all tomorrow morning" said Jimmy. "I got all these calls from customers needing me and I'm not even there to make any money." "So does she know what you do?" says Kyle. "No man she doesn't need to know right now I'm not ready to tell her everything about me yet."

Kyle and Raheem laugh at Jimmy, "ok man I'm 100% behind you if you're serious about her then I got your back. You said in two weeks is the party?" "Yes, she will be 16 June the 19th and I want this party to be special for her. Mimi I would like for you to help Terri with getting it all setup." "I would love to help out Jimmy, so is it going to be a sweet 16 party?" asked Mimi. Kyle and Raheem start laughing, "Listen I just want the party to be special for her, something that she will never forget, I'm out of here because y'all got jokes." Jimmy hugs his family and leaves the hospital.

"Hello" says Jimmy. He knew it was Nook on the other end of the phone so just to be smart he asked, "who this?" "Who this? What you mean who this? Jimmy are you coming through to spend some time with your daughter?" Jimmy looked at the phone with a look on his face, "listen Nook I told you before I will see her when I get the chance, it won't be on your time either. Stop calling me asking am I coming to see her. I told you I need a blood test before I do anything" said Jimmy. "I made the appointment for this week to take the blood test Jimmy." "Ok so when was you going to tell me, the day of the appointment?" "It's this Friday at 10am Jimmy, all you need to bring is you ID." "Ok I guess I will see y'all on Friday." "Jimmy you think that I would tell you that she's your daughter and it's not yours?" "Nook I told you that if she's my daughter I have no problem in taking care of her or coming to see her. But don't think that I will be coming to see her late nights or even spending the night at your house with her."

Laughing, "You have no idea do you Jimmy? I will need help with her at night as I will in the day" said Nook. "What your little girlfriend will have a problem if you spend the night with your daughter?" "She can come spend the night with me and my little girlfriend anytime I want her to" laughs Jimmy. "That little girl better not come anywhere near my daughter Jimmy and I mean that." "Oh, she will be around her trust me, and if she is my daughter and you want me to be in her life then my girl will be in her life. That little girl is going to be my wife one day" says Jimmy and hung the phone up.

CHAPTER TWO

"Hello, Jimmy come around to the park so you can see if you like what we did for Lisa" says Terri. Jimmy walks around to OD Park, his eyes light up "she is going to love this" said Jimmy as he gave Terri and Mimi a hug. "I'm taking her out to the movies so that way everyone can show up and we will be back around 9 o'clock when it gets dark out."

Jimmy pulls up to Lisa's house, he gets out of the car looking sharper than ever. He rings the doorbell. Lisa answers the door with this light blue slim fit back out one-piece jumpsuit on with light blue stilettos on and a light blue purse. Jimmy looked at Lisa like she was dinner tonight, his eyes was like WOW!!!!

Jimmy had on a baby blue pair of Polo Jeans with a white striped baby blue Polo shirt and a pair of baby blue Polo boots. He took Lisa by the hand and led her to the car that he had just got detailed. Jimmy opened the car door for Lisa and closed it as he was staring at her as he walked around to the driver side of the car.

Lisa was looking at him too like this brother look so good right now. Jimmy gets in the car and turns the music on, Aaliyah's song "I Care for You" comes out of the speaker of the nicely cleaned car. Lisa starts singing the song, Jimmy looking at Lisa as if he is seeing a different side of her cause she was singing the song to him. After the song was over Lisa started laughing, "what's the matter?" she asked. "Nothing I see that you're not shy around me anymore." They have been talking and hanging out with each other for three months now. "I'm getting to know you a little bit more" says Lisa with a smile on her face, that smile of hers and her eyes turned Jimmy completely on.

After the movies Jimmy told Lisa he had a surprise for her. As he was getting close to Marshall and Green Street, he told her to close her eyes. Close my eyes Lisa thought to herself like what does Jimmy have up his sleeve? So, Lisa closed her eyes and she felt the car stop. "Don't open your eyes please" said Jimmy as he got out of the car and closed his door. He opened up her door and said "keep your eyes closed" as he led her into the park. The music started playing and the song "Playa Cardz Right" by Keyshia Cole and 2Pac came on. Lisa opens her eyes, and everyone screamed Surprise!!!! Jimmy took Lisa hand and walked her to the middle of the dance floor, and they danced and sang the song to each other as they looked into each other's eyes.

"Jimmy this is so sweet of you to give me a birthday party, with my favorite colors, all my favorite foods, my family and friends are here, your family and friends are here." Lisa's dad walks up touches her on the shoulder. Lisa turns around and tears started rolling down her eyes as she hugged her mother and father. "Mom" as she cried, she looked at Jimmy, "how" is all she said hugging her mom. "Happy Birthday baby girl" Jimmy said. "Lisa we just wanted to be here when you got here to tell you happy birthday" said her father. "I'm going to take your mother back home and stay with her until your sister comes home from work tonight. You enjoy yourself and remember what I told you before young man." "Sir I just want Lisa to be happy and have a good time at her party" said Jimmy. "I promise that after the party I will take her home and make sure that she will get into the house safely." Nigel shook Jimmy's hand and Jimmy gave Lisa's mother a hug, "nice meeting you Miss Tanya" said Jimmy.

"Hey, you must be Lisa" says Raheem. "Girl you do look good, spin around so I can see what you are working with." "Lisa this is my best friend and my brother Raheem, we've been friends since we were kids." "Lisa put her hand out to shake Raheem's hand, Raheem put his arms out for a hug, happy birthday Lisa." Kyle walks over, "Happy Birthday Lisa right", "yes and thank you" says Lisa. Terri and Mimi come over, "girl Happy Birthday" says Terri as she gives her best friend a hug. "Happy Birthday" says Mimi as she also gives Lisa a hug. "Guys thank you for all the decorations, food and everything else."

The ladies take Lisa away from Jimmy, "She will be back before the party is over" said Terri as she looked at her brother laughing. "You will be alright without her for a little." Jimmy kisses Lisa on her forehead, "have fun baby girl."

"Okay bro I see you, she's a cutie and looks like she 16 if not younger." "That's my baby y'all I love everything about her, the way she walks, talks, her eyes, the way she smiles and even the way she cries. I will do anything for her." "Come on man lets go get a drink at the bar, wait is she allowed to drink?" "That's just it, she doesn't drink, or smoke. She's perfect Raheem I'm telling you she is more than a man can ask for. She's very intelligent to be her age, she's strong in a lot of what she has to deal with.

Her mom has cancer and she's there to take care of her at the age of 16." "Look man if that's what you want again, I stand 100% behind you" said Raheem, "yes big cousin I also stand 100% behind" says Kyle.

DJ puts on another record for Jimmy as he pulls Lisa close to him and sing "Fire" to her by Subway. He whispers in her ear. "I have been thinking about you all day." The music is softly playing, the gang each grabs a girl and they start slow dancing to the song. "You bring me joy from all this pain the feelings are all the same. I don't care how old we are because love doesn't have a limit" Jimmy sings to Lisa as he looks her in her eyes and kisses her on her forehead. "Lisa, I care about you a lot and I will do anything for you or your mom. Y'all dont't have to want for anything I got the both of y 'all." Lisa kept slow dancing not knowing what to say back to Jimmy.

The song ends and Lisa tells Jimmy she was going to her house to see if her sister came from work. Terri calls Jimmy over to her and tells him that Nook is here in the park and she's looking for him. Jimmy looks around for Nook. "What are you doing here?" asked Jimmy to Nook as he grabs her by the arm. Nook starts laughing, "get off of me" as she yells at Jimmy and pulls her arm away from him.

"You give this little girl a party but can't even come and see your daughter." The music stops and everyone is now looking the direction of the argument. "I told you Nook you're not my girl and if you want me to come sees her you need to give me a blood test. If it comes back that she is my daughter, you know I would have no problem in coming to see her. But I won't spend the night with her like I told you before. If you want me to spend time with her it will be on my time not yours and it will be at my house not your house" as he got up in Nooks face yelling.

Terri walked over and asked Nook what was the problem. "No problem here Terri" as her and her girlfriend walked off the basketball court and got in the car and drove off. Lisa had left while all of the drama was going on. She went to go check on her mother. When she got back, she saw Jimmy snapping. Raheem and Kyle were trying to calm him down. She ran over to Jimmy, "what's wrong Jimmy? Is everything ok?" He didn't want to really tell her what happened, but he made a promise to his self that he wasn't going to lie to her about anything.

"Nook came to the party tripping about me giving you a party and not coming to see the baby. She wants me to come and spend the night with her and the baby and I said no, if she's mines I will see her on my time not her time and if she wants me to stay with the baby then the baby would have to come to my house. Listen we are here to have a party not to worry about that psychopath" Jimmy says. Terri, DJ turn that music back on Doug E Fresh blows through the speakers in the park, the crowd starts singing the sing as they dance to the music. The park was packed with family and friends and everyone was having a good time.

"Hello", Jimmy answered his phone without looking at the number and it was Nook. "Just know that you will be sitting behind bars tonight Jimmy, so tell your little girl goodbye" and she hung the phone up. Kyle asked who was on the phone from the look on Jimmy's face he knew the call was serious. "That was Nook, she said I was going to Jail tonight so tell my little girlfriend I said bye." "Bro what in the heck have you got yourself into dealing with this girl?" "Man, I slept with her twice and both times I was drunk, it's no relationship between her and I. That's why she's mad. I really don't trust this girl man." "Well if she wants you to take care of your daughter then why does she want to get you locked up?" "Because I'm not with her."

The party was almost over, Jimmy asks Lisa if she would take a ride with him to Philly. She agrees but she has to make sure that her sister was at the house with her mother before she can leave. Ok we will stop pass there before we go.

So as they were cleaning up and people were telling Lisa nice party and Happy Birthday, Nook rides back to the park this time she has eye contact with Lisa. She called Lisa a name and kept on driving up the alley. Lisa laughed, "Jimmy your baby mom doesn't know me like that so please handle her cause I can't afford to get into no trouble behind this girl." See Lisa has a dark past too that she has not told Jimmy about yet. Lisa got into a fight in her school in Chester, some girls tried to jump her, and she put the one girl in the hospital and badly beat the other girl and charges were filed against Lisa when she was 14 years old.

"Baby girl you don't have to worry about her I'm not going to let her do anything to you." "Jimmy trust me I'm not worried about that girl" Lisa said as calm as she could and walked away. Jimmy ran up behind her and grabbed Lisa by her arm "baby girl what's up? I'm not messing with her Lisa if that's what you think, I don't want her. I slept with her twice and that's it, I was drunk both nights Lisa." "No Jimmy it's not that," Lisa paused for a second, she looked Jimmy in the eyes and said Jimmy "I got in trouble in Chester Middle School when I was 14 years old. I beat the one girl really bad and sent the other to the hospital and they kicked me out of the school. It was all over a boy that I didn't even know who he was, and his girlfriend and her friend tried to jump me. I got off because my dad is a big man in Chester, and they respect him. I got off by doing community service for 100 hours.

Nook pulls up and jumps out the car and runs toward Lisa. Jimmy grips her up and pushes her to the ground. "What's wrong with you?", Jimmy said as he was standing over top of her. Nook gets up. "You're my problem Jimmy!" as she slaps him in the face. Terri runs over and starts fighting Nook. Jimmy and Kyle pull them apart. "Don't you ever put your hands on my brother Nook because he doesn't want to be with you or your daughter." Nook trying to get out of Jimmy's grip to get Lisa. "Let her go Jimmy if she wants to fight let her go." Lisa takes off her shoes. "Little girl you don't want it with me I will trash you right here in front of everyone." Lisa laughed and told Jimmy to let her go. He let Nook go and Lisa trashed her in five seconds and walked away grabbing her shoes.

Nook got up with her face bleeding and tries to go after Lisa again and Jimmy stops her. "Listen Nook go ahead Lisa doesn't have time for this it's her birthday and she's not trying to fight you. She doesn't even know you and you come starting with her cause I don't want to be with you. It's not her fault. I made that choice not her and you come here at her party tripping and got beat up twice and you still want more. Go home to your daughter Nook. Tiffany come get your girl and take her home." Lisa was pacing back and forth upset still ready to fight some more. Tiffany tells Nook, "come on get in the car you can catch her another day." Lisa runs up to the car and tries to pull Tiffany out of the car while punching her in her face. Tiffany tries to start the car, but Lisa had a hold of her hair.

"Let go of her hair Lisa" said Terri as she tries to pull Lisa off of her. Nook runs over to the car like she was about to do something. Lisa turned around to swing on Nook, but Jimmy grabbed her. Tiffany speeds off. Raheem looked at Lisa and said, "you got a little killer on your hands bro" and everyone starts laughing but Lisa, she was very upset. Jimmy asked Lisa was she alright because Lisa was pacing back and forth. "I'm good it is just that I don't want to be fighting over you Jimmy. I don't know what this girl is up to. I am not the one to watch my back Jimmy, I will hurt that girl and her friend."

"Baby girl I'm not going to let anything happen to you. But why did you tell me to let her go if you didn't want to fight her?" "Because I had to let her, and her girlfriend know that I'm not the one to play with." So, as they finish cleaning up the crew says their goodbyes. Raheem gives Lisa a hug and tells her Happy Birthday again. "Youngin' listen my lil brother is really feeling you. He's going through these problems with his baby mom because he doesn't want to be with her. She's going to be a problem, but I know my brother is not going to let anything happen to you." "I know Raheem, thank you very much", as she gives him a hug goodbye.

Jimmy takes Lisa home. Lisa's not ready for the night to end with him. "Go check on your mom and make sure your sister is there before we leave" says Jimmy. Laura comes to the door as Lisa was about to put her key in the door. "Hey young lady Happy Birthday" her sister says and gives her a hug. "Thank you", "who's that you in the car with?" asked Laura. Lisa's older sister was very overprotective over her so they wanted to make sure she wasn't around the wrong people. Lisa grew up in a rough neighborhood where she got into a lot of trouble hanging with the wrong friends. Although she never did drugs and she was still a virgin, she had occasionally had drink beer and liquor before.

"Oh, that's Jimmy" says Lisa, "ok I want to meet him" says Laura. Lisa walks out to the car. "Hey, my sister wants to me you." Jimmy gets out of the car. He walks up to Laura and extended his hand out' to shake her. "Hi, I'm Jimmy nice to meet you, Laura right?" says Jimmy. "Yes", says

Laura, "if you don't mind me asking, exactly how old are you?" "I'm 18" said Jimmy.

"Laura dad already met him, and both dad and mom was at the party tonight, so you don't have to worry about nothing I will be alright." Laura kisses her baby sister on her forehead and tells her to have a good night and don't get into any trouble. "Lisa, I know dad had a talk with you remember what he said", says Laura. Lisa smiles at her sister, "ok mom #2" as she laughs and gets into the car.

As they pull off Jimmy turns the music on and New Edition song "Can you stand the rain" is playing clearly through the speakers. Jimmy starts singing to Lisa, Jimmy has a nice voice Lisa thinks to herself. He holds her hand as he is blowing this song out of his mouth to Lisa. Jimmy's face is really serious as he clutches her hand real tight with his. Jimmy pulls the car over and looks Lisa in her eyes and asked her can she stand the rain. Will she be there for him like he will be there for her. "Yes, I can stand the rain Jimmy and I will be there for you." Lisa is finding out that Jimmy really shows emotions through songs and him singing to her. She wonders if he does this with every one, he deals with she thinks to herself. The next song plays, and Jimmy starts to kiss Lisa on her lips. Lisa tenses up as she thinks to herself will this be the night that I will lose my virginity.

She kisses Jimmy back; he looks at her and tells her that he loves her. Lisa didn't know what to say back so she didn't say anything. "It's okay" says Jimmy "I know you feel the same way" as he laughs to himself. "How do you know how I feel Jimmy?" asks Lisa. "If you didn't have any feelings for me at all Lisa you wouldn't have been hanging out with me for these last three months." Lisa laughs and smiles, "I do love you Jimmy, to be honest with you Jimmy you're the best thing that ever came into my life.

Can I ask you a question?" "Sure, anything you want baby girl." "I notice that you show your emotions through slow songs, do you do that with all the girls, that you been with like Nook?" He turns and looks at Lisa but still trying to keep his eyes on the highway. "Lisa, I have been with a lot of girls and I'm always going to be honest with you. I never fell in love before. It was always sex with them and that was it. I would get drunk and you know most if not all people get horny after they drink. So, it would be one-night stands and if I want to hit it again I would but again it was nothing but sex with all of them. This is why Nook is acting the way that she's acting. After I hit that twice I left it alone I never called her again. She would show up at places that I was at, and I would act like she's not even there and she would get mad."

"Lisa I never asked you to have sex with me, right? I would only kiss you on your forehead, right? Tonight, was the first night I kissed you on your soft lips. And yes, they are soft" laughed Jimmy. "No" said Lisa "you didn't, but yet I'm still here with you, I just told my sister and my family in Philly that I was going to marry you and they laughed at me. But I am serious. The way I feel about you I have to keep you in my life. I'm not going to ever have these feelings ever again about anybody. So, this is why I show my emotions through these slow songs cause that's how I truly feel about you."

Jimmy has a little condo in downtown Philadelphia which no one knows about but Raheem and Kyle. Soon Lisa will know about it too. They meet up with Mimi, Raymond and Kyle to finish the rest of Lisa's birthday out. They go to this club in Center City. As the night went on it was getting late, it was now after 3am and Jimmy knew he had to take Lisa home. "Hey guys we have to go" said Jimmy, "I have to get Lisa home." Mimi gives Lisa a hug and tells her goodnight. Kyle extended his arms out, "come here little cousin in-law" and he gives Lisa a big hug. They get in the car and the music cuts on and the Isley Brothers is playing Spend the night. Jimmy really meant what he was singing to Lisa especially with this song. He heads toward 76 and Lisa says, "Jimmy I will spend the night with you tonight." Jimmy asked, "Are you sure?" "Yes, I don't want this night to be over" says Lisa. Jimmy takes Lisa's hand and kisses it as he turns his car around and heads to downtown Philadelphia.

Lisa is looking around like where we going so she asked Jimmy. "We are going to my condo", "you live down here in Philly." "Yes, I've been living down here since I was 16 years old." 16!!! Lisa was surprised and thinking to herself why he was not living with his mother or father. They pulled up to the condo, "oh my god Jimmy you were living here when you were 16 years old." Now Jimmy knew he had to talk to Lisa about what he was into how he got this condo and the nice car he was driving at the age of 18.

As they walked up to the front door Lisa was looking around saying to herself this is a nice neighborhood compared to where she was from. Jimmy opened the door and they both walked in. As Lisa was walking in, she didn't know what to think. She looked around, the ceilings were very high, and the kitchen was done nicely. He also had a fireplace in the living room. Jimmy showed Lisa around. Her eyes were so big to what she was looking at in the beautiful three-bedroom, three-bathroom condo. He also had a deck in the master bedroom. "Jimmy your house is really nice and it's clean." He laughed, "what did you think I'm some dirty dude?" "No, I just didn't think someone your age would live like this." "Well that's because I'm barely here." "So you just pay rent to somewhere that you don't stay at?" "Baby girl here sit down. Lisa growing up my dad sold drugs all of his life while all of my uncles sold drugs too. My mom didn't have to move to Norristown, but she did after my dad got killed. I got into a lot of trouble growing up to the point I was put away at 12 years old." "What happened? Why they send you away?" "I don't want to scare you off Lisa, but my cousin Marcus got into something with a couple of guys and I shot the one guy." "Did you kill him?" "No but he was hurt so bad that I had to go to an all-boys camp. I stayed there until I was 14 years old. I came home and Kyle and myself was out on the steps at my aunt Nae's house and these guys tried to rob us. We also keep our piece on us no matter what because that's what we were taught from our dads. So anyways we later caught the guys and we beat them with a baseball bat. Kyle and I both did 15 months in a Juvenile Detention Center. I came home and my dad got killed two days after, my mom was not having me out there selling drugs or getting into trouble, so she left me down here to stay with my aunt and uncles."

"How did your dad get killed?" asked Lisa. "He was shot, drug deal gone bad, but my uncle Timothy is spending a life sentence in jail because he killed the man that killed his brother. Lisa, I sell drugs, a lot of drugs. I also help my dad's company build houses every now and then just to keep the feds off my back. So, I will work for them six months out of a year and that's how I really get my money. The drug money I stack away and use the paycheck from them to pay my car note and the taxes on this condo." "Oh, so you own this?", "yes I got my GED and graduated from this school my aunt sent me to this year."

"Even if I was to get locked up for selling drugs, I have enough money right now to last me for the rest of my life. My dad had a healthy insurance policy and due to him and my mother wasn't never married the money went to Terri and myself. We both get a check every month for the rest of our lives." "Oh wow" said Lisa, "I guess my life doesn't compare to yours at all." "Tell me about your life" Jimmy said, "it's nothing, I stayed in fights growing up because a lot of the girls in the middle school I was going to thought I was messing with their boyfriends. The boys at the middle school were all cool and we were friends and that was it. Yet because they were jealous of me, they would try to fight me. My sisters, and my brother Derris and myself were put in a boxing class when we were three years old. He is born and raised in Chester, so he knew that we were going to have some problems living there. I told you tonight what happened when those two girls tried to jump me in the 6th grade. I have stayed out of trouble since then. And you know my dad owns his own construction company as he told you, he already owns four hotels so I'm like you set for the rest of my life."

They both laughed, Jimmy turned on some music and sat down beside Lisa. "You want anything to drink?" he asked her. "No thank you" says Lisa. "You like you some slow music don't you" asked Lisa. "My boys laugh at me cause that's all I listen to is slow music. They have meaning to all of them" Jimmy says. Lisa tells Jimmy that she was tired and asks if she can lay down because her head was spinning. He walks her into his bedroom. Lisa takes off her clothes. Jimmy looks at her beautiful body but still says in his mind that he is not going to sleep with her yet.

Lisa starts singing the song that's playing, "Softest Place on Earth" by Xscape was playing. Jimmy is quiet as he listens to her beautiful voice sing. Lisa asks Jimmy if he wanted to be the first in the softest place on earth. Jimmy laid down beside Lisa fully dressed. He pulled her close to him and just held her. "Lisa, I do want to be the first but not tonight. I respect your father and I promised him that I will wait until the right time comes." As the music plays Lisa starts kissing Jimmy. She unbuttoned his pants and starts kissing him on his neck. Jimmy grabs her hand and looks at her and asks if she was sure this is what she wanted to do.

Another song comes on and Lisa whispers, "Jimmy I like this song" as she sings "Stroke me up" by Changing Faces. Jimmy laughs "so now you feel the slow music too." "Jimmy I always loved slow music because that's all my mom listens to." Lisa just kept singing while taking off the rest of Jimmy's clothes as Jimmy softly says he don't mind. She pulls him on top of her as they made passionate love to each other. Jodeci's song "U & I" came on and Jimmy whispered "this will be the song that I'm going to sing to you when we get married", as he made love to her he kept on singing and Lisa was loving every bit of Jimmy's soft body inside of her.

The next morning came about and Jimmy was woken by his phone ringing. Lisa was still in his arms as he answered the phone, "hello" said Jimmy without looking at the number. It was Nook on the other end screaming in the phone, "it's messed up Jimmy that you would let your little girlfriend do that to your baby mother" as she cried in the phone. Jimmy looked at the clock and it was 6am. "Listen girl you put yourself in that predicament when you came around to her party starting with her. Why haven't you scheduled the appointment for the blood test yet Nook?" "You are not getting a blood test" she screamed in the phone, "you will never see your daughter again." "Ok" said Jimmy and hung the phone up. He pulled Lisa closer to him as he held her real tight in his arms.

It's now 8am and Lisa wakes up, "Jimmy I have to go home and check on my mother, my sister left already for work." "Ok baby girl I will take you home, let me grab some clothes so I can take a shower at my mom's house."

On the ride home Lisa tells Jimmy that she loves him and last night was a night that she would never forget. "And what did you mean when we get married? Do you even know that we will be together that long?" asked Lisa. "We will be, I'm not going nowhere Lisa, everything I say and sing to you I mean it from the bottom of my heart. You're very special to me and I mean that. You know things about me no other female will ever know. No one knows about my condo but my sister, Mimi, Kyle, Raheem and now you. I never took a girl there ever, that's our house baby girl and whenever you're ready to move in the door is open, matter fact here is your set of keys to the condo."

They pulled up to Lisa's house. Lisa gives Jimmy a kiss and tells him that she loves him, "love you too baby girl. I will call you later, I'm going down to the hospital and see my cousin after I get dressed so I will stop pass here before I go down there." "Ok I will see you later" Lisa said as she gets out of the car.

Jimmy calls Kyle, "hey what's up man?" "nothing about to get dress and head on down to the hospital so I can give Mimi a break. Her and Raymond went there last night after we left the club." "Alright bro I'm about to get dressed myself and head on down there I will see you soon."

After Jimmy got out of the shower, he called Lisa, "hey baby girl what's up?" "Hey Jimmy", says Lisa with a smile on her face blushing. "Baby girl you were awesome last night. I think I'm falling in love with you more and more" says Jimmy. Laughing Lisa says, "don't say things you don't mean", "oh I mean every word I said. I'm almost done getting dressed" says Jimmy, "about to stop pass and see you before I head to Philly."

Nook is block riding Marshall and Green Street because she sees Jimmy's car parked in front of his mother's house. Jimmy comes out of the house and Nook pulls up on him. "Jimmy your daughter wants to see you." Jimmy walks toward the car. When he gets close enough Nook sprays him with mace and pulls off, "MY EYES!!!!" screams Jimmy. Ms. Lynn which is his mother's neighbor runs over to Jimmy and takes him in her house and washes his eyes out with cold water. "Thank you Ms. Lynn"," who was that?" asked Miss Lynn as she passes Jimmy a towel to clean his face. "That's some girl that claims I'm her baby's father but won't give me a blood test."

Miss Lynn and Jimmy's mom is the best of friends and she looks out for Terri and Jimmy when she's not around. "Baby mama drama huh, sweetie you better be careful with this girl because she is a little crazy" laughs Miss Lynn, "I saw the whole thing." Ok Miss Lynn I will be careful, "Thank you again for your help," Jimmy goes back over to his mom's house to get his glasses and walks over to his car. He sees that Nook scratched Narlyn real big on the side of his car. Jimmy is heated now. He calls Nook and she didn't answer the phone. Jimmy gets into his car and drives to Nooks house. He jumps out of the car and kicks Nook's door in and starts punching on her. "Call the cops!!!" screams Nook. Tiffany called the police. When the police arrive, Jimmy was getting into his car. "There he go right there" cries Nook, "he kicked in my door and started beating on me."

"Get out of the car sir" said the officer, Jimmy gets out of the car. They handcuff him and put him in the back of the cop car. Someone had called his sister down there. Terri comes running around the corner. "What happened?" she asked the officer. She looks at Nook and asked" what happened here?" Jimmy yelling out of the cop car window, "she mace me and scratched her name on the passenger side of my car Terri." The police officer takes Jimmy out of the car so they can hear his side of the story.

"Listen this car pulls up in front of my mom's house and tells me that this child that is supposed to be my daughter wants to see me. I walk over to the car and she pulls out this mace and maced me. My neighbor next door to me witnessed the whole thing. I look on the other side of my car and she scratched her name big as day on my car." This is the side of Jimmy nobody has ever seen but his family. Nook see's nothing but fire in Jimmy's eyes. She was laughing inside cause now she knows how to push his button and that's exactly what she will be doing until he starts coming around his daughter and her.

"Is she your daughter's mother?" asked the one officer. "Sir I asked her over and over to give me a blood test, she hasn't done it yet, but yet she keeps harassing me about coming to spend time with her and her daughter." "I want to press charges on him, he kicked in my door and put his hands on me screamed Nook." "Please calm down ma'am" one of the officers said. After the police got both sides of the stories, they took the handcuffs off of Jimmy. Jimmy pulled $150 dollars out of his pocket and gave it to Nook and told her to get her door fixed.

"Terri, come on get in the car" said Jimmy. As they were driving off Jimmy told Terri he was going to get their cousin Kyla to trash Nook. "I'm going to bring her and her girls up here and show her where Nook lives, and she knows what to do from there. I'm tired of this girl. All I'm asking for is a blood test and then I will take care of Narlyn if she is my child. This is what this is all about. No she wants me to spend the night at her house to spend time with the baby. I told her no, if she's my child I will come and get her, and she can spend the night with me I don't have to stay at her house just to spend the time with her. And she freaked out, you not taking my daughter nowhere if you want to spend time with her it will be here at my house with me. Terri, I looked at this girl like she was crazy, I guess I will have to figure out a way to get this blood test on my own. Cause this girl is not trying to take a blood test, she knows that the situation will go a different direction than what she plans." "So, what are you thinking about doing?" asked Terri. "Well I will give her what she wants, I am going to buy one of them blood test kits and I am going to go and spend the night with Narlyn. I am going to swab both mine and her mouth and then send it off to be tested."

"What about Lisa? Jimmy if she finds out you will hurt her." "Terri I am going to tell her everything I'm about to do. I told Lisa I will never hide anything from her, nor will I lie to her about anything." "You really care about her", "yes I told you I am going to marry her."

Jimmy drops Terri off at home and heads over to Lisa's house. He knocks on the door. Lisa answers, "hey baby girl", says Jimmy with this sour look on his face. "Hey what's up", asked Lisa as she looks at the way his face is looking. "Baby I have something I need to talk to you about." "What is it?" They sit down on her steps in front of her house. He starts with taking off his glasses and turns to look at Lisa. "Jimmy what happened to your eyes?" asked Lisa. "When I was at my mom's house getting dressed Nook called and said that she was outside, and she wanted me to see the baby. I walked up to the car and that's when she maced me in my eyes. The lady that lives next door to my mom took me into her house and washed out my eyes. After that I looked at my car and saw that she had carved Narlyn on the passenger side of the car big as day. Lisa, I flipped when I saw that and went to her house and kicked in her door and started punching on her. Her girlfriend called the cops on me and they had me in handcuffs ready to lock me up. Terri came down there and after that they took me out of the car heard my side of the story and let me go."

"Wow so this girl is going to be a problem I see." "Well it's all because she wants me to come to her house and spend time with the baby and her like as if we were in a relationship. Lisa, I have no feelings for this girl at all. I told you I slept with her twice and that's because I was drunk. I didn't even know the girl was pregnant until she was eight months. This is why I keep asking her for a blood test cause I'm not sure if the little girl is mines."

"But anyway I have an idea that I want to talk to you about first." I will go to her house and I will stay there but I'm going to swab Narlyn's mouth while I'm there and send the kit out to get tested to see if she's mines." Lisa looks away from Jimmy with hurt in her eyes, she knows Jimmy but she doesn't know Jimmy. They have been dealing with each other for five months now.

He grabs Lisa hands, "baby girl I will never hurt you I'm not going there to spend the night with Nook, I'm not evening spending the night at all." "What do you mean Jimmy?" "Listen I'm a tell her to hop in the shower like as if we are going to do something and while she is in there, I will swab Narlyn's mouth then mines. I will package it all up and bounce." "Isn't that going to make her come at you more Jimmy?" "It will, but at least I will have control over where I can spend time at with Narlyn."

"Ok Jimmy" says Lisa "I guess I will have to trust you." She puts her head down thinking is he telling her the truth or what. But I guess I would have to trust him until he shows me otherwise Lisa thinks to herself. Jimmy sits in between Lisa's legs. "Lisa I'm not trying to hurt you, nor will I ever hurt you. I love you I am going to marry you when you turn 18. Lisa, I promise you that." Jimmy gives her a hug and kiss before he leaves. "I will see you later tonight, I have to take my car up to New York to my boy's shop."

"Raheem owns an auto body shop in New York" Jimmy tells Lisa. Tears are in Lisa's eyes as she tells Jimmy ok, she will see him later. He hears the crackle in her voice and turns back. He walks up to her and holds her in his arms as tears fall down Lisa's face. "Hey, hey" says Jimmy 'listen" as he lifts her face up to look at him. "Lisa, I don't want Nook if I wanted her I would still be messing with her. Lisa you don't have to worry about nothing I don't want anybody but you. We will be together for the rest of our lives mark my word." He pulls her hand down to where his private area is and tells her this is what happens every time I come near or around you. "This been like this since the first day I met you, so I know for a fact I'm not leaving you for anybody because no one ever had me feeling like this, no one Lisa."

Jimmy blows a kiss to Lisa as he gets in his car and pulls off. Lisa wipes the tears that are falling from her eyes as she walks in the house. "Mom what are you doing up?" asked Lisa as she helps her mom into the kitchen. "Baby I'm ok I feel fine today, was that Jimmy you were out there talking to?" "Yes, it was", Lisa says with a low voice. "Baby what's the matter?" her mom asked as she looks at Lisa. "Nothing I'm ok mom", "here sit-down Lisa" her mom looks at her. "Sweetie I'm your mother I know when something is wrong with you so tell me what's going on." "Mom, Jimmy might have a daughter." "Wait what do you mean he might have a daughter?" "Well when I first met him at the party in the park he was all over this girl named Nook, I asked Terri was they dating and Terri told me no. She was just someone he slept with before and she has been in his face ever since he slept with her. She got pregnant and never told him until she was eight months. She called his phone the day he took me to meet his family in Philly and said that she needed him to take her to the hospital. He told her that he wasn't in town, then he asked why she had to go to the hospital, and she said that she was in labor. He asked why she was calling him shouldn't she be calling the baby's dad. She said you are the baby dad, so she had the baby and now she won't give him a blood test."

"Mom she came to my party starting with me." "Lisa baby what did you do?" Lisa put her head down, "mom I gave her what she wanted, and I tried to walk away but she asked for it." "Lisa honey you know you can't get into any more trouble. They have you on probation until you turn 18 Lisa." "Mom I know but she asked for it, her and her girlfriend." "Lisa what did you do to the other girl?" her mom asked her. "Nothing really I just tried to pull her out of the car while I was punching her in her face." "Sweetie your lucky no charges were pressed on you." "No I don't think that's what it's about mom. I think she wants to intimidate me but when she seen that I wasn't scared of her she has been coming at Jimmy. She maced him earlier today and carved her name on the passenger side of his car. She knows I'm the only one that's in his car and I would see it. She wants him to be with her. She told him that in order for him to see the little girl he has to come to her house and see her."

"So, Jimmy thinks he should go there, act like he's going to spend the night with them and take the blood test his self. He's going to swab the baby's mouth while Nook is in the shower. After he does it, he is going to leave." "He doesn't think that it isn't going to cause more problems with her after he does that. He knows thats he will cause problems, but he said that if the little girl is his at least he will be able to take the little girl when he wants to." "Do you believe him?" "Yes, and no" as she looks at her mom with tears in her eyes. "Mom, daddy cheated on you and it separated the whole family. I'm not ready for that." "Baby you can't take what happened with your father and I to your own relationship. Jimmy really loves you Lisa give him a chance he might not be lying. Try to trust him before you just think that he is lying." Lisa gives her mom a hug, "I love you mom you always know what to say to make me feel better."

"Hello" answered Raheem. "Bro I'm on my way out to see you, Nook carved her name on my car in big letters man. I wanted to kill that girl man. I will explain it to you when I get there."

"Hello", answered Kyle. "Bro I will be down there at the hospital after I drop my car off to Raheem. This girl messed my car up and maced me bro. She's mad cause I'm messing with Lisa for one. I asked this chick 10 times to give me a blood test and she still hasn't done it but thinks I am supposed to come and spend the night at her house to spend time with Narlyn. I'm going to go get one of them kits that they have at the drug store and take the blood test myself." Kyle laughing, "man how did you get involved with that girl anyway?" "Drinking that's how man, and now I'm paying for it" said Jimmy. Kyle laughing, "ok man I will see you when you get down here be safe driving up there", "got you", says Jimmy.

Jimmy pulls up to the auto body shop and Raheem walks up to the car. "Man, she did a job on your car" said Raheem. We have to buff that out and paint it bro." "That's fine", said Jimmy. "I just need a car to get me around until you are done with mines." "So, what happen? Where did all this come about?" says Raheem. "Man, this girl thinks I should be with her to see Narlyn. I asked her over and over for a blood test, she keeps giving me the run around. I'm not going to be in that little girl's life if she's not mines Raheem. I'm thinking about going to her house acting like I'm going to spend the night with them. I will tell Nook to take a shower like we are about to do something and when she goes and gets into the shower, I'm going to swab Narlyn's mouth then mines. After that I'm just going to up and leave. Man, she's not going to have control over me because a baby is involved."

"She called my phone while I was getting dressed at my mom's house and tells me to come outside she wanted me to see the baby. I go out there walk up to the car and this girl maces me right in my eyes man. The neighbor had to wash my eyes out, then after that I come out to get in my car but you know me I had to walk around the car because I know what I'm dealing with and I see this on the side of my car. Now you know I seen nothing but fire right, man I kicked her door in and started beating on her like she was a dude. Tiffany was trying to pull me off of her, so she called the cops on me. But you can tell Nook was liking that I was hitting on her. Man her face was like yes he loves me. The cops came and they had me in handcuffs but let me go. I gave that girl $150 to fix her door and left, like I don't have the time for that crazy girl.

Jimmy heads back to Philly to visit his cousin. "Marcus is doing a lot better" said Mimi, "he's sitting up in the bed and he's talking." "What's up little cousin?" said Jimmy to Marcus as he gave him a big hug. "I'm in some pain but I'm glad to be alive, what happened to the guys that did this to me?" asked Marcus. "Man, we not going to discuss that right now" said Kyle. "We just want you to get better and come home." Marcus knew what that meant they took care of them, "say no more" as he smiled at his brother and big cousin. They did take care of the problem but there is one more that they didn't get but he got locked up on some other charges. Raheem murdered all three men one by one, when he was about to take the other one out, he got locked up for robbing the corner store around their way.

CHAPTER THREE

yle pulled up to the house with Marcus, since he was released from the hospital today. "Surprise" screams the family as Kyle brings his brother in the house. "Hey baby brother" says Mimi as she gives him a big hug. "Little brother", says Jimmy "welcome home man". Jimmy takes Lisa's hand, "Marcus I want you to meet my future wife, Lisa this is my little cousin and brother Marcus", "hello" says Lisa. "Ok Jimmy she is cute" said Marcus, "how old is she?" "She looks young". Jimmy smiles as he takes Lisa and walks off so she can meet his aunt and uncles.

All the family is at the welcome home party and Lisa fits right in; everyone loves her. Raheem calls and lets Jimmy know that his car is ready. He couldn't make it to the welcome home party cause his twin daughters were having a birthday party that day. "Hey baby girl you want to take this ride with me to New York, Raheem just called me and said that my car is ready." "Yes, I will go" says Lisa as she puts a smile on her face thinking to herself my baby is looking real fine.

On the drive up to New York they talk about if Narlyn is Jimmy's daughter how would Lisa feel about that. "Jimmy I'm here with you all the way, like you said you got my back I will have your back. I know that she is going to give us problems I see that already" says Lisa. "But can you handle that?" asked Jimmy. "Nook is a piece of work but Jimmy she's not my problem, long as she stays in her lane we are all good cause I can't get into any trouble." Jimmy looks at Lisa, "why do you keep saying that is there something I should know about you that you're not telling me?" Lisa looks at Jimmy and says, "I'm on probation until I turn 18 Jimmy, the judge told me if I get into any more trouble that they will take me away from my mom until I turn 18 and it might go into jail time all depends on the charges." "I will keep her away from you as much as possible, Lisa I want to stop selling drugs, I want to marry you and start a family with you." Lisa looks at Jimmy and asks if he was sure that's what he wants, "Lisa all I know is that I want to spend the rest of my life with you."

They pull up to the garage, his car is sitting in the front with a note on the window, stop pass the house before you leave out to go back to Philly the note says. He parks the other car on the side of the garage with all of the other cars. They pull up to Raheem's house which is in Up State New York. Lisa's eyes are like this house is amazing. The gates open up and they drive up the driveway. Jimmy gets out of the car and opens the door for Lisa. Lisa is still amazed on what her eyes are looking at. Raheem has a four-bedroom, four-bathroom house. Nice backyard with a pool. My brother yells Raheem as he walks out to greet Jimmy and Lisa. "Hey Lisa" as he gives her a hug, "nice to see you." "Come on in the party just started", "Jimmy what's up my brother" says Brick. Brick is another one of the guys that grow up with them, but he never comes to Philly unless he has to. And if he has to come there you know that there was a big problem that Jimmy or Raheem couldn't handle. My man Brick says Jimmy, "so who is the lovely lady you got here Jimmy?" "This is Lisa my baby girl and one day she will be my wife" expresses Jimmy, "Ok Lisa welcome to the family" said Brick.

"Uncle Jimmy!!!!" Brittany runs and jumps in Jimmy's arms, Brittany is Raheem daughter and one of the twins. Raheem has three kids. The twins Brittany and Briana who the party is for and he has a baby boy that is three months old and his name is Raheem Jr. "Hey baby look at you all grown up on uncle Jimmy", the twins are five years old, uncle Jimmy screams "Briana" as she also jumped into his arms. Lisa smiles as she sees how Jimmy interacts with the girls. He's going to be a good father she thinks to herself. "Ok girls let uncle Jimmy go say hi to your mom." Bianca, walks over and gives Jimmy a hug, "how have you been?" "I'm good, hey this is Lisa, Lisa this is the mother of Raheem's children", Lisa extended her hand to shake Bianca's hand. "Lisa you want to follow me out to the yard" says Bianca, as they are walking through the house Lisa is amazed as to what she is looking at. "Your house is beautiful", "thank you, Jimmy and Raheem did all the work in the house and the backyard." When they enter the yard, it has a big swimming pool in it, nice size deck, fire pit with chairs around it, a bar with seats and a high-end grill with a lot of food on it.

The kids were having so much fun in the pool. "Hey how's Marcus doing?" "You know he came home today, we told him that everything was taken care of and that he has nothing to worry about. And as far as the other one he will be locked up for a while, plus if he was to get out, he has enough people on his head right now we don't even have to do anything. He hopes he makes it through a month in jail without someone taking him out in there" says Jimmy as they both laughed.

Bianca introduced Lisa to everyone at the party, Lisa felt at home, just one jealous girl out the bunch, and that was Tina. Tina always did like

Jimmy; she was another one that he slept with two times and never called her back because he didn't have any interest in her at all.

Tina kept staring at Lisa with a stink look on her face. Bianca walked over to Tina, "hey what's up with you why you are looking like that?" "Who that girl over there sitting with Jimmy" asked Tina. "Oh, I believe that's his girlfriend, she's cool. I like her for Jimmy, she looks like she has him a little calm, he just looks and acts a little different then the last time I seen him."

See the other fellows in the crew were all older than Raheem and Jimmy, but Jimmy had the brains, he started the trin with the drug selling. A lot of the guys took their profit and brought store fronts, garages to fix cars, the one opened up a laundromat so the feds will stay off their backs. Jimmy will work for his dad's company six months out of the year just to have an income while he puts the drug money to the side. The guys have been dealing drugs since Jimmy was 14 years old. Raheem is a year older than Jimmy and he has it made; he has his autobody shop that is the best in Up State New York. A nice big house, and he sales cars. Brick owns a seafood store and a sweetshop. Jimmy wants to own his own contracting company, so he doesn't have to work for his dad's partner anymore.

Jimmy sees Tina watching him, so he puts his hand on Lisa's butt and pulls her real close to him. He gave her a kiss like he was making love to her. Lisa asked what was that all about Jimmy. "No reason I just love you that's why", he looked Tina's way and smiled, she was mad, she took her sons hand and told Bianca she had to leave something came up. "Man, why do you always make that girl mad like that?" said Raheem as he was shaking his head laughing. "I told that girl plenty of times I don't see her that way and she just think every time I come out here that things have changed. I saw the way how she was looking at Lisa, my baby has nothing to do with how these chicks feel about me, and they give her dirty looks and want to fight her for no reason, and she doesn't even know them."

Lisa was 5 foot 7, caramel complexion mid back straight length hair, a body to die for at the age 16, because a lot of the girls wanted Jimmy or he slept with them once or twice and never called them again they didn't like Lisa for that reason. Jimmy was fly he was 5 feet 9 chocolate dip nice clean cut, with facial hair nice and trimmed and the women loved him. He always stayed dressed and everything he wore matched his complexion and that is what made him so sexy.

Bianca walked Tina to the door, "girl why do you put yourself through this you can't get mad at the chick she doesn't even know you or anything about what happened with y'all two. Just forget about him because he clams this one here as his soon to be wife so you know she not a one-night stand, and I think this girl is really changing him. And don't you talk to Ron anyway, why you still on Jimmy. I thought Ron and you were in a relationship." "Bianca we are but I fell in love with Jimmy." "Wait" said Bianca "you fell in love with him and y'all only had sex two times so how you fall in love with someone that you only been with them twice?" "I can't explain it" says Tina, "when Ron and I are together I wish that he is Jimmy." "Well you need to get over him because the way I see it girl he is happy with the shortie he is with now. Anytime he says she is going to be his wife then he really loves that girl. You know Jimmy as long as I knew him and you never seen that man with one girl. Look girl you all caught up in your feelings with Jimmy and he doesn't even want you." Tina looked at Bianca with a tear in her eye, "you right I do need to get over him this is why I need to leave B, I can't be around him and to see that he walked into your yard with another girl is bothering me." Jimmy and Lisa walks through the kitchen heading for the front door, Jimmy gives B a hug "ok sis I will see you the next time I'm up this way." "Nice meeting you" says Lisa as she looks at Tina while walking to the door. "Tina nice seeing you again tell Ron I said what's up and sorry I missed him this trip around, hope to run into him the next time I come out this way."

Jimmy opens the passenger side door for Lisa and he gets into the car U & I by Jodeci comes on, the car is gliding down the road as the music blows through the speakers and once again Jimmy is singing to Lisa telling her that this will be their wedding song. That ending part of the song just touches Lisa because she can feel that he is serious about he loves her. Jimmy takes Lisa shopping while they are in New York. She asked him to ride by the Paradise Inn which is the new hotel that her dad is building.

CHAPTER FOUR

Lisa just turned 18 and Jimmy is ready to propose to her. Him and Terri goes out looking for a ring that he knows will brighten his baby girl eyes up. They found the perfect ring now Jimmy wants it to be the right time to ask her, they have been together for two years now and he couldn't wait for her to be of age where he can spend the rest of his life with her. Jimmy puts together a dinner for his soon to be bride for her 18th birthday.

Lisa just thinks it's a dinner for both families so everyone was there from Lisa's side and Jimmy's side of the families. The dinner was held at the fire house in Conshohocken, everyone was having a good time, the DJ get on the mic and asks Lisa and Jimmy to come to the middle of the dance floor. Lisa looks around like what is going on, Jimmy walks over to Lisa looking sexy as ever. He had on a pair of blue jeans, white sneakers, and a polo white t-shirt. He extends his hand for hers; she's looking at him "Jimmy what is going on?" They walk out to the dance floor and the DJ plays Lady I love you by O'Bryan, they hand Jimmy the mic, he sings the song to Lisa and at the end Jimmy gets on one knee and say "Lisa I love you pulls a little blue box out of his pocket takes the ring out, takes Lisa's left hand and asks "Lisa will you marry me?" Tears are running down her eyes as she says yes. Everyone stands clapping and crying, Terri walks over to her best friend, "ok Jimmy you can let her go", Jimmy laughs and says no as he is still holding Lisa in his arms. Sike he kisses Lisa in her lips baby" I will see you later", Lisa shows Terri her ring, "girl I know I went to pick it out with him last night". "So, you knew all about this Terri? You my best friend" "and I'm his sister you think he was going to ask someone else to help him look for your ring?'

Everyone walks over to see Lisa's ring, her ring was blinging and the rock on the ring was big. "Hey mom", says Lisa as she gave her and her dad a hug, "mom I 'm so glad you made it out." Lisa's mom is not doing too good, but she made it to see her daughter graduate from high school. She kissed Lisa on the cheek, "I'm so proud of you baby girl you are going to make a good wife and mother once you have children."

"Hello" Jimmy says to Nigel, "let me talk to you over here." Nigel shakes Jimmy's hand, "I know you will make my baby happy I see the glow on her face every time she's around you. Jimmy, her mother is not doing to good right now, she is hanging on just for Lisa, I ask that you make sure that my daughter will be taken care of if when her mother is called home. Lisa will take owner ship of the hotels in King of Prussia and in New York. I want to know what you are going to do with your life now that y'all are engaged." "Sir I was talking with Lisa and I think I'm going to take you up on your offer to go in business with you at your construction company."

"Sounds good, so did y'all set a date for the wedding?", "yes it will be on her 19th birthday. She wanted a summer wedding, sir I promise to give your daughter the world. I will never leave her side." "I trust you Jimmy, well her mother and me are going to get out of here and let y'all have a nice night." "Lisa I'm going to take your mother back to Chester with me so you and your sisters can have a good time." "Love you mom", as she gave her a kiss on the cheek, "thank you for coming dad love you."

Nook found out that Jimmy proposed to Lisa and now she's been harassing him even more. Although Jimmy finally took the blood test and found out Narlyn was his, Jimmy has been going through a lot with Nook to see his daughter. Narlyn is now three years old and only seen her dad three times. Nook has taken Jimmy for child support. She told the judge that he sells drugs and doesn't work. Nook was very upset that Jimmy showed the Judge his pay stubs that he has from the company that his dad was partnership with. Jimmy is two steps ahead of Nook in everything that she is trying to do to him, she is trying to keep him away from Lisa.

The birthday party is over and the couple is on their way driving back home, "Hello" says Lisa as she answered her phone, "Lisa Lisa!!!!" screamed her sister in the phone. "Come home now please", Laura was crying. "It's mom Lisa come home, mom is in the hospital." Lisa bursts out in tears. "Jimmy, please take me home they rushed my mother to the hospital. But by the time they got to the hospital Lisa's mom has passed away. Lisa broke down into her sister's arms. No!!! why she cried, they sat her down Jimmy took his fiancée into his arms and held her close to him as tears rolled down Jimmy's eyes.

Jimmy why she cried, Lisa got up and ran to the bathroom holding her mouth as if she was about to vomit. Leaned over the toilet Lisa starts vomiting and crying at the same time. Linda comes in the bathroom behind her, "Lisa are you ok?", in between breaths Lisa says "yes". Lisa grabs her stomach, Linda I'm in a lot of pain please help me my stomach is really hurting.

Linda runs and gets Jimmy to help Lisa from the bathroom. Jimmy runs, "Lisa what's the matter?" "Jimmy my stomach is hurting really bad she says as her head is held in the toilet." Laura comes running in with a doctor, they put Lisa in a wheelchair and rushing her to one of the beds in the emergency room. They run all types of tests and found out that Lisa was eight weeks pregnant. Jimmy is smiling once Lisa woke up. "Jimmy what's going on, why am I in the hospital?" Jimmy kissed Lisa, "baby girl we are about to have a baby", tears rolled down her eyes. "My mom would have been a grand mom Jimmy", "Lisa you have to calm down. Baby the doctor wants to talk to you." "Hi, my name is Doctor Brice, we ran some tests, your blood pressure is very high, however congratulations Ms. Thomas you're eight weeks pregnant.

Now according to the tests that we have ran on you it looks like you can be at a high-risk pregnancy. We're going to keep you over night for observations with your blood pressure. I know you're dealing with the loss of your mother right now but we need for your blood pressure to go down. The doctor left the room, "Lisa this is a blessing from mom. Mom is in a better place right now, she's not in any pain anymore and plus she left you with a baby to bring into the world", said Linda.

Jimmy spends the night with his fiancé at the hospital, they talk about her mother and the baby. "Lisa your sister is right your mother was in a lot of pain I know all she wanted to do was to see you finish school and baby girl you did that. If you want to go off to college, I will watch the baby. I will have your back baby all the way in anything and everything that you want to do." "Jimmy, I know that you will have my back and I thank you for that." Lisa phone rings, "hello" it's Lisa's dad, "sweetie how are you doing?" "I'm doing good dad my blood pressure went down and I'm going home sometime today." "Great" says Nigel, "I need to get all of y'all together to discuss the funeral service for your mother." Tears started coming down Lisa's eyes, "daddy I can't do this right now, whatever decision y'all make I'm ok with it. I don't want my blood pressure to go back up", "ok baby girl I will talk with you later."

Today is the day that Lisa and her family will lay her mother to rest. Jimmy has his fiancé by the hand holding it tight, Lisa barely can walk she's crying and it's hard for Jimmy to calm her down. When they got to the grave site Lisa lost it. She tried to climb in the ground with her mother as they were rolling the casket down in the ground. Linda and Derris tries to take Lisa to the car. "No!!!" she cries falling to her knees. Terri is hugging Jimmy as he is crying because his fiancé is crying, and he doesn't know what to do. Once they got her in the car Jimmy gets in the car and holds Lisa. "Jimmy my mom is not coming back, why?" is all she says crying. "Baby your mom would want you to carry on with your life, you have a person growing inside of you that your mother is smiling right now. As your mother was called home a new life will enter into this world 7 1/2 months from now, but you have to stay calm." Lisa calmed down she laid her head across Jimmy's lap; the service was over, and everyone got into their cars. "Jimmy, I don't want to go to the repass I want to go to your house in Philly, I need to get away right now."

They get to the Carver Center and Jimmy tells Lisa's sisters that he is taking her to his house in Center City. He gave them his phone number and address if they needed to get in touch with Lisa or for any other reason. Jimmy also lets Lisa's dad know what's going on, "yes take her down there until she's ready to come back home Jimmy. Right now, I need for you to watch over her, she needs you right now", said Nigel. "Lisa and her mother were very close, she's going to probably need someone to talk to Jimmy, wherever her mom went she always had Lisa with her from the time Lisa was born. They were very close with each other, very close," "sir I will make sure that Lisa will be good and if she needs to talk to anyone, we will go together so she can get all the help that she needs." "Jimmy thank you for taking good care of my daughter, her mother would have been happy."

When Lisa and Jimmy get to Jimmy's house Lisa goes into the bedroom and lays down. Her head is spinning, and her emotions are all over the place. She tries to go to sleep but she keeps thinking about them lowering her mother's casket in the ground. Tears starts running down her eyes as she starts crying harder, Jimmy walks in the room bringing Lisa a glass of water and sees that she is crying. Jimmy lays down beside her, he holds her tight and Lisa lost it, Jimmy rocks her until they both fell asleep.

Lisa phone rings and it's her dad, "hey daddy", "hey baby girl how are you doing?" "Dad I will be alright; Jimmy has been here talking with me and helping me get through this hard time. How are you holding up?" "I'm ok I know that she's not in any more pain and I don't have to see her suffer anymore." "How is the baby doing, are you taking it easy Lisa?" Tears coming streaming down her eyes, "yes daddy I'm taking it easy I don't want to lose my baby so I'm trying really hard to just think that mom is watching over us and that this little person inside of me was a blessing from God." "Yes, it was so please take it light and take care of yourself, I will call you tonight or tomorrow, lay down and get some rest", "ok I love you dad."

Lisa curls back up into Jimmy's arms and falls asleep. Ring ring, "hello" answers Jimmy, "so I hear that you proposed to your little girlfriend and y'all about to have a baby. Narlyn is three years old and you don't even come and see her or do anything for her." "Nook listen when I bring stuff to my daughter you either throw it away in my face or cut it up in my face. So, until we go to court, she will not get nothing from me. You want me to come to your house so you can try and say I slept with you or so you can start an argument with me so I can put my hands on you.

"Jimmy, I don't want you I just want you to spend the time with your daughter." "Nook I don't have to spend the night at your house just to spend the time with my daughter, she can come to my house or I can take her to my mom's house." "My daughter is not coming around that little girl, and she will never be a sister to that thing you and she are about to have." "Ok is there anything else you want to say because I'm not going to get into it with you, I will save it for the courts."

Jimmy has recorded all the conversations with Nook and saved all the text messages so he can bring them to court. Narlyn had to go to the emergency room last week because she fell down the steps and her mother was nowhere around when it happened. He also has the paperwork from the police station and the hospital. He knows that he is going to have problems with her, he's trying to keep Lisa away from her as long as he can so she can have a healthy baby.

Jimmy goes to see his cousin Marcus. "Hey little cousin, how are you feeling?" "I'm doing good man." "Auntie, where's Kyle at we have to take this ride to New York? He will be right back. He took Kayla home. All man I missed my little lady again."

Kyle named his daughter after his twin sister Kayla, she's two years old. "Jimmy I was talking with Jule's brother and he said that the boy that they locked up the police found out that he had something to do with Jules' murder. Apparently when Jules was coming home from the corner store the boys approached him and one of them pulled out a gun and started shooting. They asked his brother did he have anything to do with the killing of the other three men that was involved." Jimmy just looked at his cousin thinking that the heat is off of them and is on Jules family. "Boy about to do life over trying to rob somebody and end up with a murder charge" said Jimmy.

"Anyway, I hear you got a little one on the way", says Marcus, "yeah man and I am so excited. Marcus Lisa is the best thing that came into my life. I told her that I really want to stop selling drugs and get into the business with her father." "Oh, ok", says Marcus, "what kind of business is he into?" "Construction, he has five hotels already that him and his crew built. I'm already working for the company that my dad was part owner of. But if her father is offering me part ownership of his empire why not take it" says Jimmy. "Yes, why not", said Marcus, "and Lisa the baby, and Narlyn are all of the reasons why I want to get out of the game", says Jimmy. "Go for it bro you are still young; look at Raheem he is almost out of the game himself, he has a lot of property that he owns so he really don't need to sell drugs anymore." Jimmy just sat there thinking how his life would be if he was out of the game. "Brother" says Kyle as he walked into the kitchen reaching out to Jimmy and shaking his hand. "Yo we have to make this run to New York", said Jimmy.

Jimmy and Kyle head out to New York to link up with Raheem and Brick. They pull up to Raheem's house and Jimmy sees Tina sitting on the side deck with Bianca. "Uncle Jimmy", the twins run up to him, then they run to Kyle, "uncle Kyle" as they jump into his arms. Raheem comes out the house shakes both Jimmy and Kyle's hand. They head to the den which is Raheem's office. The men sit, drink and talk about what is their next move. Bianca knocks on the door, "come in" says Raheem, "baby I put some food on the grill for y'all", she gives the men hugs and walks out the room. Before she closes the door she tells them I made some sides also to go with the meats so if anyone is hungry.

Jimmy really didn't want to sit out there with Tina because he knows that Tina has this thing for him. They all walked out on the deck sat, drank and talked and laughed. The whole time Jimmy felt Tina looking at him, his phone rings and it's Lisa, "hey baby girl" he says. "Everything ok?", "yes, I just wanted to hear your voice" says Lisa, "and wanted to make sure that you made it to New York alright." "Yes, we made it safely", "ok I love you" says Lisa "call me when your leaving", "ok I love you to baby girl, how is my little one doing?" Jimmy says with a big smile on his face. "The baby is fine I'm Just laying here getting as much rest as I can." "Alright I will call you later", he blows a kiss at the phone before he hung up. Tina put her head down because she knew the person that Jimmy was talking to was his girlfriend.

I have a toast to make so fill your glasses up as I make this toast. "To my brother, best friend and #1 man, I know you're going to be the best husband and father to Lisa and the baby" says Raheem. "And I can't wait until the day you say I do", Tina gets up and walks off the deck, she goes to the bathroom and begins to cry. Tina and Jimmy only been with each other twice and Jimmy never called her ever again, but always ran into her at Raheem's house because her and Bianca were best of friends.

Tina gathers herself together before going back outside with everyone. "You okay?" asked Bianca, "yes, I will be fine", as she puts her glasses back on so no one will see that she was crying, especially Bianca. She didn't want her to ask questions. The men are into a deep conversation about the wedding, Bianca is trying to talk with Tina, but Tina is really not paying attention to her. She's upset because Jimmy never called her or even acknowledged that she is in the same backyard that he is in. Tina is trying to hold it together but she's in love with Jimmy.

Raheem was making more drinks and he asked Tina if she wanted a drink. Tina's mind was somewhere else so she didn't hear him the first time he asked her. "Girl what is the matter with you?" asked Bianca, Tina said nothing and told Bianca that she had to go. Bianca walked Tina to the front door, she looked at Tina and tears were rolling down her cheeks. "Girl you have to stop this, Jimmy is about to get married and have a baby, so you have to get over him plus Tina you're in a relationship with someone. And how did you fall in love with someone that you only had sex with twice?" asked Bianca.

Tina starts crying, she sat on the sofa, "B you just don't understand" she cries. "I don't understand. What do you mean? What I do know is that I can't see how a person falls in love with someone when only being with that person two times. I think you're in love with the sex. He must have put that thing on you", laughs Bianca. "B it's not funny", cried Tina, it might only have been two times, but they were special to me. "Well Tina I really don't think it was special to Jimmy, so you need to get over him."

Bianca talked Tina into coming back in the yard, she watched Jimmy throwback them shots of Hennessey. See Tina knows that's how her and Jimmy ended up having sex the two times that they did because Jimmy was drunk. But this time Jimmy tells Raheem he has to leave so he can go home to his wife. Tina was furious with Jimmy and got up and walked past him almost knocked him over as she switched out of the backyard. Raheem looks at Jimmy, "man she is heated with you", "I don't know why I wasn't never in a relationship with her and never will be in one with her." "Jimmy she's really in love with you says", Bianca. "I tried to talk to her and ask her how she fell in love with someone that she's only been with two times in her life." "Bro I'm out of here I will get up on y'all later", said Jimmy as he laughed and shook his head walking out of the gate of the yard.

"Jimmy can I talk to you?" said Tina as she was leaned up against his car. Kyle's face was like "oh wow" as he got into the car. "What's up?" asked Jimmy. "Why haven't you called me Jimmy? You think it's ok to treat a woman like that." Jimmy looks at her, "girl you know what it was the first time we did it, I was drunk we went into the guest room and that was that. You didn't have a problem with it then so why do you have a problem it now. And the second time we did it I was drunk again, and you came on to me that trip around.

"Listen Tina I really didn't mean to hurt you if I did, I didn't want to lead you on so I apologize if I did. Tina it was nothing but sex that's it, I'm in love with someone else that's about to have my baby and I'm going to marry her. Again, I am sorry for what your feelings are", tears started streaming down Tina's eyes, Jimmy gives her a hug which that was a big mistake, Tina bit onto his neck so hard Jimmy had to slap her for her to let go. Kyle jumps out of the car and pulls Tina back as she tried to run up on Jimmy for smacking her. Raheem, Brick and Bianca comes running out of the backyard because they heard yelling from Tina. "Jimmy you will pay for this you not going to get away with treating women the way you do", as she cried and jumped into her car and pulled off.

Jimmy is holding his neck, "did she break the skin?" Jimmy asked Kyle. "A little bit, man I think you should go to the hospital when we get back to Philly and get a shot man." "Jimmy what happened?" asked Bianca. She was out here by my car and she asked me if she can talk to me. "She was crying so I gave her a hug and she bit me on my neck. I guess she thought that I would get in trouble because I have a bite mark on my neck." The men started laughing, "Raheem what is so funny?" asked Bianca. Soon as he got into the car, he called Lisa and told her what just happened. "One thing he will not do is lie to that girl", said Raheem. "That's my baby", said

Jimmy, "why lie to her, she's the only one I will not lie to". Jimmy said as he was about to pulls off. Kyle gives Bianca a hug and gets in the car.

Jimmy and Kyle pulled off, Bianca looks at Raheem and says, "why you can't be more like Jimmy and love me the way he loves her?" "Wait this isn't about you and me", Raheem starts laughing. Brick laughs and says, "yo man I got to go", he gets into his car shaking his head as he left them in the driveway arguing. Raheem has another child by another girl, and the baby is nine months old, Bianca just found out about the baby a month ago. "Bianca I'm not going to sit out here and go back and forth with you, I'm not Jimmy." "So, are you saying that you don't love me Raheem?" "I'm not saying that but what I am saying is that this conversation is over with", as he walked in the house going to the den closing the door behind him.

"Hello", answered Lisa. "Hey baby I'm leaving Raheem's house now, I need you to go to the hospital with me when I get back to Philly." Jimmy told Lisa what happened from the beginning, how he slept with Tina two times and how she was obsessed over him. "So that's why she didn't speak back to me when I spoke to her that day we were up there." "Yes, she said I treated her bad because I never called her back. I told her that she knew what it was from the start that it wouldn't be anything between us but sex. Anyway, I'm on my way home, I'm dropping Kyle off and coming home." "Ok I will see you when you get here", says Lisa.

CHAPTER FIVE

Three months have gone by and Lisa is now 5 1/2 months. Linda, Laura and Lisa are at her mother's house cleaning out her mother's things. Derris was away at college for his last year of Business Management. The ladies got everything all cleaned out and are taking it to Goodwill. "Hello", answered Lisa as her phone rings. "Hey baby y'all done?", "Yes" "How are you feeling about all of this?" "Jimmy it was hard, but I know my mother wants me to be happy that she's not in pain anymore. I know that she is watching over us. I'm actually good right now." "Ok baby girl I was just calling to check up on y'all, call me when you're ready to come home and I will come and get you." Jimmy had a surprise for his soon-to-be wife. He wants it to be an early wedding gift. Jimmy brought Lisa a brand new royal blue Lexus car with tinted windows. "If you look at this car you would think that Jimmy bought it for himself", Kyle says to Mimi. Jimmy and his family was close so whatever they did they do it with each other. So, everything he wants to do for Lisa he has to have either his sister Terri or his two-girl cousins Kayla and Mimi to help him out with it.

Jimmy wants to make sure Lisa has everything she can imagine having; she will have the car the house and the kids. Jimmy signed all the paperwork, gave Kyle the keys to his car and they drove back to Philly. He parked Lisa's car in the garage and Kyle parked Jimmy's car on the street. "Jimmy she's going to be so happy once she sees this car", said Mimi, "yes blue is her favorite color and she just got her license her last birthday."

Jimmy had cooked for Lisa before he left out to go pick her up from Norristown. He called Lisa and told her that he was on his way, "ok I will be ready" says Lisa. "Linda help me up off the floor please", Linda laughs, "girl you are getting big, you sure it's only one baby in there." "Yes, it's only one baby." Jimmy should be pulling up any second, Lisa made her way down to the living room while her sisters were laughing at how she is walking now. Lisa is so big right now but she's only 5 1/2 months.

Jimmy pulls up in the nicely cleaned royal blue Lexus car. He gets out and leaves the door open for Lisa to get in. Lisa looks at him, "Jimmy baby what are you doing? What happened to your car asked Lisa?" Linda and Laura were standing in the door. Laura whispered to Linda "I love that car, it is so clean" says Linda. Jimmy put the keys in her hand, Lisa this is an early wedding gift from me to you. Lisa started crying, her sisters came out to give her a hug and to see the inside of the car. "I love the inside", her sisters said. Lisa gives Jimmy a big hug and a kiss. "I love you baby", says Lisa "thank you for the car. "LET'S RIDE" says Lisa, Jimmy laughs as he gets in on the passenger side of the car, Lisa beeps the horn to her sisters, and they drive off.

"Jimmy this car rides nice and smooth I love it." "Yes, baby I knew you would that's why I got it for you." Jimmy has a black Lexus just like the one he bought for Lisa. He told Lisa he wanted his and hers matching cars, they both laughed as she got onto I-476 heading to Center City.

They pull up to the three story condo and Lisa smells food. "Was you cooking something before you left because it smells so good?" The dining room table was setup for two, "Jimmy you cooked?" asked Lisa, "yes I did", as he pulled out the chair for her to sit.

"Baby that food was very good, I didn't know you knew how to cook. Jimmy feel my stomach the baby is kicking." Jimmy looks into Lisa eyes as he rubs her stomach, "I love you so much, I love and I'm in love with you", he says as he starts to kiss her.

Jimmy puts some soft music on as he carries his soon to wife to the bedroom, Troop- "All I do is think of you" is playing, Jimmy is singing to Lisa as he is making passionate love to her. He whispers in her ear, "I will never leave you Lisa, I will never lie or cheat on you, I love you." "I love you too" says Lisa.

They both cuddle up into each other's arms and fall asleep. There's a knock at the door, Jimmy looks around and wonders who can that be because no one knows where he lives but his boys. He looks at the phone, there are no missed calls, Jimmy grabs his gun out the top drawer and walks into the living room. He peeks out the window and sees that it's his next-door neighbor. "Hey Carl, what's up?" asked Jimmy. Carl was drunk, he ended up at the wrong house again. Jimmy takes Carl back over to his place, tells his wife that he went to the wrong house again. "Thank you, Jimmy" said Carl's wife as she closed the door. Jimmy went back into his condo. His phone is ringing, "hello" said Jimmy. "Jimmy your daughter wants to see you, she has been crying for you." "It's 12 o'clock in the morning Nook why is she up?" asked Jimmy.

"Listen Nook I'm not around to come and get her. I will come and get her for the weekend." "Jimmy my daughter is not going anywhere with you and that little girl. If you want to see her you have to come here and see her." "I'm not coming there, you maced me, you tried to run me over, you scratched my car up so why would I come to your house? Listen I don't put my hands-on females but that's what I think you like, if I can't take Narlyn with me then Nook I guess I will not be seeing her then." as Jimmy hung the phone up.

The next morning comes and Jimmy tells Lisa that he's going to Norristown to try and get his daughter without a fight with her mother. I'm taking Terri with me so hope there will be no problems. He kisses Lisa and heads to Norristown, he calls Terri to see where she is, "Jimmy I'm sorry I won't be able to go they called me in to work today." "That's alright sis I will be fine," "ok call me and let me know how thing went."

Jimmy gets to Nook's house and he parks his car three blocks away from her house. Jimmy knocks on the door, Nook answered the door with nothing on but a long T-shirt. "Hey, I come to get Narlyn is she ready?" "No, I have to get her dressed, you can come in and wait though." Jimmy hesitated before he went in the house, he has his phone already on record ready for whatever Nook has up her sleeves. "Jimmy, Narlyn just fell asleep and I don't want to wake her up", "oh ok I will come back later to come get her." "Jimmy can we talk for a minute?" "Nook we really don't have anything to talk about, I just came to see my daughter and take her out for a couple of hours." "Jimmy all I want is you to be a father to your daughter." "I'm trying to be a father you already know that I'm in a relationship and about to get married. You keep coming at my fiancé for nothing she has nothing to do with this, she doesn't really even know you Nook." "I heard you are about to have a baby with the little girl." "Please stop calling her a little girl" says Jimmy. "Her name is Lisa and yes we are about to have a baby in three more months." Jimmy can see the steam coming out of Nook ears, so he chuckles a little bit before standing to his feet walking to the door. Nook puts her hand on the door as she stands in front of Jimmy and starts to rub on his private area. Jimmy pushes her hand off of him and says, "call me when Narlyn wakes up" and walks out the door.

Jimmy calls Lisa and tells her what just happened. "Lisa, I think I'm just going to wait until we go to court, this girl is something else and I don't have the time for this. She actually came to the door with a T-shirt on like I was supposed to say ok let's take it to the bedroom. Baby girl I'm on way back home, I was going to wait for Narlyn to wake up but I'm just going to wait for us to go to court." "Yes, I think that's the best way to go about it" says Lisa "because if she is going to be tripping like that then yes let the judge handle it." As Jimmy gets on the 476 his phone rings and it's Raheem, "hey man what's up?" "Hey Jimmy man listen Bianca just told me that Tina pressed charges on you for smacking her." "What? This girl is tripping, let me take a picture of my neck since she wants to play like that. I really don't understand why shorty acting like this over two nights of nothing but sex. She acts like I asked her to marry me and have my babies. I'm also going through a lot with my baby mom. I just came from Norristown trying to see my daughter and this girl comes to the door with just a T-shirt on, and as I was leaving, she starts rubbing on my private area." Laughing Raheem says, "serious man". "Yes, Raheem like I pushed her hand off of me and walked out the door, she told me that my daughter was asleep when I got there I guess she thought we was going to do it or I don't know what she was thinking but it didn't happen."

The court date came for Jimmy and Nook for joint custody of Narlyn, the judge granted that the two will split custody of Narlyn. Since Jimmy lived in Philadelphia and Nook lived in Norristown, Jimmy will have his daughter every weekend. Narlyn was in daycare in Norristown and Jimmy agreed to pay for the daycare. Nook wasn't going for that, she jumped up "my daughter is not staying with him and that little girl that he is living with. My daughter will not be a big sister to that ugly baby that she is about to have. If he can't spend time with his daughter where she lives, then he will not see her at all", yells Nook.

"Order in the court", the judge yells, "Ma'am you need to calm down, if you don't I will grant full custody to the father." Tiffany tried to calm Nook down, Nook was crying and it was hard for Tiffany to calm her down, but Nook ended up calming down. Lisa is sitting there looking at Nook acting crazy, Lisa kind of chuckled to herself, this fool is crazy she thinks to herself.

Nook turns around and starts talking trash to Lisa. Lisa looks at her like girl please but if you come over here, I will put you on your back again. "Little girl please don't let me see you in the streets". "The judge said to Nook Ma'am one more outburst out of you I will hold you in contempt of this court."

Jimmy is sitting there watching Nook, he says with a low voice this girl is nuts. The judge gives Jimmy and Nook papers to sign of the agreement he made, he told Jimmy to sign his first and he can take his daughter and leave. He told Nook that she will need to wait for them to leave and then she can sign her paperwork. Nook was furious, hurt and upset, not only that she's not taking Narlyn home with her today, but that Jimmy brought

Lisa to court with him and Lisa is now seven months and big as I don't know what.

They strap Narlyn in her car seat and drive off, Jimmy knows he will have to keep these two ladies apart from one and another. He doesn't want anything to happen to his unborn child.

Now that this case is over, I have to go up to New York and take care of the one with Tina. "When is that court date?" asked Lisa. "Tomorrow morning at 11AM. Lisa I will need for you to watch my daughter for me." "Baby that's not a problem I would love to get to know this cute little girl. They pull up at the condo, Jimmy takes Narlyn out of the car, she smiles at her dad, Narlyn really couldn't speak clearly at the age of three. Nook never took the time to teach her how to talk, go to the potty or how to eat with utensils.

Later that night, Lisa is giving Narlyn a bath and notices how dirty the water was. She thinks to herself when the last time was this little girl took a bath. But she didn't say anything to Jimmy she just kept it to herself and thought I'm going to raise you as if you were my own child. Lisa took her out of the bath and dried her off. Narlyn smiled at Lisa grab her face and kissed her. Oh, sweetie Lisa said as she hugs her, Jimmy walks in the room and sees that his daughter is loving his fiancé which puts a smile on Jimmy face.

"Jimmy your phone is ringing", says Lisa as she is putting pajamas on Narlyn before she puts her in her bed. Jimmy and Lisa went shopping for his daughter a couple of weeks ago. He wanted to be ready for his daughter when she came to visit.

The next morning came and Jimmy was getting ready to go up to New York to deal with the charges that Tina filed against him. He had Lisa take pictures of his bite on his neck because he knew this was going to happen. He knew the way Tina was hurting that she was going to try something like this.

Jimmy gets to the courthouse and was waiting to see if he seen Tina come in. Jimmy walks in the courtroom and does not see Tina, he thought to himself this girl is tripping. How do you file charges on someone and don't show up in court? "Jimmy Smith", he hears his name being called, "yes that's me" as he walked up to stand in front of the Judge. "Mr. Smith I'm sorry you came all this way, but the charges were dropped on you from the complainant so you are free to go." "Thank you, sir," says Jimmy and walks out the courtroom. He calls Lisa, "Hey baby girl" he says, "why this girl didn't even show up in court Lisa. I don't know what type of games this girl is playing, I'm on my way to see Raheem now and talk to Bianca about her girl." "Ok" says Lisa, "how is Narlyn doing?" "She's taking a nap right now. I fed her, gave her a bath and laid her down for a nap." "Baby girl you're going to be a good mother to our kids", "thank you, love you and I will see you when you get home" says Lisa." Okay love you too baby girl."

Raheem is in the front yard as Jimmy pulls up in the driveway. Jimmy gets out of the car, "hey man" he says as they shake hands with each other. "Raheem that girl didn't even show up in court today." "I know" says Raheem, "she's been here crying to Bianca for an hour, saying how sorry she was to press charges on you. Bro I don't know what's going on with these women today" said Raheem as he started laughing. Raheem was ok in cheating on Bianca, he doesn't have the same feelings for her as Jimmy has for Lisa. He will be out with another woman and tell Bianca that he was in Philly with Jimmy and Kyle. Or he was in the Brooklyn New York with Brick, but all and all Raheem was out with another female cheating on Bianca. Bianca knows in her heart that he still messes with his other baby mom cause the baby is a new baby and he's always over there. She really doesn't say anything because for one she really can't prove that he is cheating because he always comes home and he also takes care of the three kids that they have together.

"Man what is up with this girl? I want to say something to her but she might press charges because I asked her a question." The guys started laughing, "Hey Jimmy" says Bianca as she gives him a hug, "Hey B" says Jimmy. "B, why your girl didn't come to court today?" "Jimmy she's in the backyard now crying, talking about how she is in love with you. She knows that y'all only had sex twice but she cares a lot about you and she didn't want to make any trouble for you. She asked me to ask you if she can talk with you." "I don't know B after that last incident I'm scared she might try something, if she wants to talk Raheem and you will have to be out in the yard with us." "Jimmy you know I got your back" laughed Raheem, "man it's not funny, I don't understand these females. Is her and Nook related?" laughed Jimmy as they walked around to the backyard.

"What's up Tina?" asked Jimmy as he sat in the seat across from her. "Jimmy, I want to apologize for last week. It's just I got caught up in my feelings for you." "Tina, I don't know how you would have feelings for me, and we were only together twice. And that was a year ago" said Jimmy. "I can't explain it Jimmy, but I been had these feeling since the last time we were together." "But Tina I have no feelings for you, besides I'm about to have a baby next month and I'm getting married next year." "I understand Jimmy I don't want to cause any problems to your wife or unborn child", she says. "So, are we good?" asked Jimmy. "Yes, we are good, can we shake on it?" laughed Jimmy, "yes" Tina reached out to shake Jimmy hand. Raheem walks Jimmy out to his car, "man that was weird, I don't trust her" said Jimmy. "She has this look like she's up to something man, I could feel her looks through her glasses, and how calm she was talking to me." Jimmy shakes his head and gets into the car beeps his horn as he drives away.

CHAPTER SIX

"**P**USH PUSH!!!" the doctor is saying as he is delivering Lisa's baby. The baby is here crying and kicking, Jimmy is excited as he cut the cord of his beautiful 7lbs 6oz 21 inches long baby girl. The baby is put on Lisa's chest for her to see her daughter before they take her and clean her up.

The nurse brings baby girl, Jymayia, in the room and hands her to Lisa but Jimmy reaches out for his daughter. He's smiling at his beautiful baby girl, Lisa's looking at Jimmy saying to herself he is such a good dad. Knock knock, it's Lisa's sisters and her father "let me see my niece" says Laura as she takes Jymayia out of Jimmy's hands. "So, you just going to take my baby from me like that" says Jimmy joking with Laura. "Jimmy let me talk with you out in the hallway" says Lisa's father. "Jimmy have you thought about what we talked about?" "Sir yes and I am going to take you up on your offer. Lisa and myself was talking and I told her that I wanted to get out of the game and work with you." "No son I'm giving you your own site that you will be the boss, the hotel in King of Prussia is the site where you will be running."

Jimmy was excited and couldn't wait to tell Lisa the good news. "But Jimmy you will need to be completely out of the game, all your money will need to be changed into clean money." "Sir that's been done, my brothers and I always cleaned our money." "Ok so give me a week and I will have everything in order for you. Now when Lisa turns 21 the hotel will be in her name; you will have other sites to run but I know this one will take a about a year to build. I see you have a little bit of architect skills so I will link up with you for the designs of the building." "That's great" says Jimmy with a smile on his face as him and Nigel shook on it.

So, it's getting closer to visiting hours to be over, Linda and Laura didn't want to give their niece back to Lisa. They give Jymayia to Lisa, kiss both of them on their foreheads before saying bye. Lisa's father gave her a kiss bye and told Jimmy that he will be in touch with him by next week. "Ok sir and thank you", "Jimmy you don't have to keep calling me sir, you can call me Nigel." Jimmy laughs and say thank you Nigel.

Once everyone left out of the room Lisa asks Jimmy what was that all about. Excited Jimmy says "your dad just offered me to be the boss of his construction site in King of Prussia. He wants me to help build the hotel" says Jimmy. "Jimmy that is wonderful news", "I told him that I'm ready to get out of the game Lisa. I want to be here for you and my kids. I don't want to be dead in a year or two or locked up for the rest of my children lives. I want to be a good father to my kids and a good husband to you." "Baby you are already a good father and husband; I love you so much" Lisa says as she kisses Jimmy on his soft lips.

It was time for their daughter to go back to the nursery, a bed was pulled into the room for Jimmy to sleep in. They stayed up most of the night talking about their wedding and their newborn baby Jymayia. "Hello" says Jimmy as he answered his phone it was Nook on the other end. "Jimmy so you want to play daddy to your ugly baby huh you need to bring my daughter home Jimmy. Who has my daughter while you out playing daddy to this other baby? I told you that I didn't want my daughter around that baby." "Nook listen, my daughter is not ugly for one, and don't worry about where my daughter is, she is in good hands" Jimmy said as he hung the phone up on her. "Did she just call my baby ugly" said Lisa? "Baby don't worry about her she is just jealous that she will never have me or her daughter for that matter, I'm taking Nook back to court and going for full custody of my daughter. Once I get everything together with your father I'm taking my daughter from her."

The day came that Lisa and her newborn baby were going home, Nook has been calling Jimmy and harassing him about their daughter Narlyn. She also was saying some bad things about baby Jymayia on Jimmy's answering machine. But Jimmy never said anything to Lisa about what the texts that Nook was sending him. He didn't want her to get into any trouble. Jimmy knew that Lisa will hurt Nook if she found out that she was talking about Jymayia.

They got home. "Ok I see someone has been doing some work around the house" said Lisa. Jimmy had put everything together in the baby's room including the rocking chair for Lisa and the baby.

Lisa was amazed how Jimmy put their daughter's room together, tears came to her eyes, the room was painted in a pretty pink with white borders, he had built some pink and white shelves in the corner where the crib was and on the shelves it was pictures of Jymayia's sonograms. Also Jimmy waited for Lisa to take naps at the hospital and he changed their daughter in three different outfits so he can take pictures of her. He had the pictures blown up and he put all of the pictures nice and neatly on the shelves. The crib was pink and white which transformed into a twin-size bed for Jymayia once she got older. She had a 50-inch color flat screen tv mounted on the wall. On the other wall he had built shelves across the wall for her sneakers on one side and her shoes on the other side. She had sneakers and shoes from size 0 up to size 5. Lisa opens up a door off to the side and it was a walk-in closet, it wasn't very big but it was big enough for his little girl. Jimmy also showed her Narlyn's room and her room was done the same way as Jymayia's room. Lisa couldn't believe her eyes Jimmy did a good job with the girls' rooms. "You like what I did?" asked Jimmy, "yes" cried Lisa as she turned to give her man a big hug and kiss.

"Baby girl I'm going to Norristown to pick Narlyn up from my mom's house, I'm going to take Jymayia with me so my mom and Terri can see her plus I want you to get some rest." "Thank you because I need to get some rest" says Lisa. Jimmy gives her a kiss, packs the car and heads to Norristown to see his mother and sister.

Jimmy gets off the Norristown exit in Conshohocken, his phone rings and its Nook. "Hello" Jimmy answered. "Jimmy when are you dropping my daughter off, she has daycare in the morning?" "Nook she will be there in a little bit, I will call you when I'm on my way" and he hung the phone up.

Jimmy gets to his mother's house, "bring my grandbaby here" says Jimmy's mom. "Oh my she looks just like you Jimmy" she says looking at Jimmy. "She looks just like us Jimmy she is so beautiful." Terri gets her and Jimmy's baby pictures, "look mom she's a spitting image of us" Terri said. "Terri let me talk to you for a second" said Jimmy as they walk out of the room.

"Listen can you drop Narlyn off to her mother for me? I just don't feel like the arguing with Nook about the baby and her keep calling my daughter ugly." "Wait what? She is calling someone ugly she has some nerve" says Terri. "She's just jealous that you and she had two nights together and Lisa and you will spend a life together." Jimmy is cheesing from ear to ear, "what you all smiles for?" laughs Terri. "Me and my baby will be spending a lifetime together. Terri, I love Lisa so much and I'm not trying to jeopardize our relationship by going to Nooks house, I know she is going to say something out of her mouth that's going to make me mad especially when she talks about my daughter. I'm not trying to go to jail because I know she will provoke me to put my hands on her. The last time I was at her house she tried to feel me up as I was trying to leave out the front door, she will try anything so she can run and tell Lisa."

After the visit with his mother and sister Jimmy gives Narlyn a kiss on her forehead and says "daddy will see you next weekend baby". Narlyn is crying telling her dad she wants to go with him. Jimmy feels bad that he has to let her go back to her mother. "Terri I will take her back just come with me if she sees that you are there, she won't try anything or even start an argument with me." "Sure, big brother because I got some words for her calling my niece ugly", "Terri no" said Jimmy. "Nook is spiteful Terri she will do anything she can to either stop my wedding or being a father to my daughters. I'm afraid that she will have me locked up before my wedding. This is why I got out of the game and going to work with Lisa's father doing construction, he's giving me my own site to run and everything Terri. I'm trying to stay away from that girl until I'm granted with full custody of my daughter." "Ok Jimmy I won't say nothing to her until you get Narlyn but after that I'm got to let her have it. She is not going to come after my brother and best friend like this and nothing is going to be said to her."

Terri and Jimmy pull up at Nook's house but they are in Terri's car so Nook wouldn't know what Jimmy was driving. Nook was sitting outside with Tiffany; Terri gets out of the car with Narlyn. "Where's your brother at?" said Nook with an attitude, "he asked me to drop her off", she gave her niece a kiss and got back in the car. As she was pulling off Narlyn started crying, "SHUT UP!!!" shouted Nook as she pulled the little girl in the house. Jimmy wanted to get out of the car and take his daughter home with him but instead he was recording Nook so he can take her back to court with him next month.

Terri looks at her brother and sees that he wanted to kill Nook for yelling at a three-year-old like that and pulling on her like she was a rag doll. When they got back to his mother's house he tells his mom what happened. "Mom I have to get my daughter out of that house. She doesn't keep the house clean; my daughter shares a room with her girlfriend she gets food stamps and never has food because she calls me every week telling me that my daughter needs something to eat. She has weed roaches in every ashtray in the house", Jimmy shows his mom all the pictures that he has taken of Nooks house. Each time he went there to get his daughter he took pictures, records their conversations so he can present to the courts. Jimmy was hurt and couldn't wait to bring his daughter home with him for good.

Lisa and his daughter have created a bond with each other, Narlyn loves Lisa says Jimmy to his mom. "She's always smiling with her, she stays grabbing Lisa's face and kissing her like as if Lisa was her mother. Lisa potty trained her taught her to eat with a spoon and fork, showed her how to tie her shoes and dress herself at the age of three, mom. When she 1st came to our house she didn't know how to do any of those things, mom but Lisa has been a great stepmother to her." Jimmy's mother looks at her son and sees that he is bothered by the situation, "Jimmy be patient God will grant you your daughter. He sees that she is being treated wrong you just have to trust in God and wait on him." Jimmy gives his mom a kiss on the cheek, hugs Terri "thank you sis. Come on little one we have to get home to mom who is waiting for us."

"Jimmy walks in the house, hey baby girl" he says as he kisses her. "What was that kiss for", "baby I love you so much and I'm so happy to have you in my life and in my daughter's life." He sits down on the sofa, Lisa notices that something is wrong. "Baby what's the matter you look irritated about something." Jimmy takes her hand please sit down he asked, "Jimmy what is going on?" "Lisa when we dropped Narlyn off to Nook she cried and her mother started yelling at her she dragged her in the house like she was a ragged doll Lisa. Tears started flowing down Jimmy's face as he looked into Lisa's eyes. Baby I got to get my daughter out of that house." He shows Lisa the pictures of the house, the ashtrays, the refrigerator with no food in it. He also shows her the room that Narlyn sleeps in with Nooks girlfriend. "My daughter doesn't have to live like this and it's all because she can't be with me. Lisa, she has been texting me harassing me about getting me locked up that I won't see the day of our wedding and that Jymayia is ugly."

Lisa's face turned a shade darker when he said what he said. "Jimmy let me have her phone number" she said angry. 'Lisa no I want our wedding to go on I know this girl will do everything in her power to stop me from being married and being a father to my children. And when we go to court and they grant me with my daughter it's going to make her even more mad. Lisa I couldn't even get out of the car to stop what she was doing to my daughter; I know if I would have got out and said something, she would have tried to put her hands on me. Terri and I would have been locked up, so I did what I thought was the right thing to do and stay in the car."

Jimmy cried to his fiancée, Lisa held him tight and cried with him. The next day Jimmy saw that it was 13 text messages on his phone and they all were from Nook sending him messages that she loves him and that she wants to work things out with him so they can be a family. Jimmy was in Philly at his aunt Nae's house, "man this girl is weird look at these crazy messages she sent me" he said to his cousins Kyle and Marcus. "First it's I'm going to make sure you don't get married to that "B" and if you can't be a father to your daughter here you not going to be a father to that ugly baby. Now it's oh I want to work things out be a family, is she crazy because for one we never were a family or even in a relationship for that matter. I slept with her two times and now we a family" all three of the men started laughing. "Her and Tina should be friends because I only had sex with the both of them two times and now they act like we was in a long-term relationship" laughs Jimmy. "Nook is happy that she got a baby out of it so that's why she thinks that we should be in a relationship."

"Hello" answered Jimmy, it's Lisa's father, he wants to link up with Jimmy so they can discuss the next move on their plans to work together. "Sure, Nigel I can meet with you this Friday, what time do you want to meet?" "Is 10AM good for you?" asked Nigel, "yes" says Jimmy, "ok I will see you then." "Hey bro what's that's all?" about asked Kyle. "That was Lisa's father and he wants me to come and work with him doing construction. He's giving me my own site to build in King of Prussia. Kyle. I want to get up out of the game, I have a family now and I'm about to get married in six months so I want to be here for my wife and children." "I feel you man, Kyle we're the only two left in the game. Raheem, Brick they all have their own business, Lisa father looking out for me with my own site is all I need. Kyle will you come and work for me, I want you out of the game too man these streets are getting ruff out here. Man we will end up dead or in jail for the rest of our lives Kyle, you have a daughter." Kyle thought about what Jimmy was saying to him and took Jimmy up on his offer.

CHAPTER SEVEN

immy and Nigel meet at Nigel's house in Chester, Lisa and Jymayia also came along so her father can see his granddaughter. While the men were talking Lisa went next door to her girlfriend's house so she can see the baby.

The men shook on the deal and Jimmy will start working on his project building the hotel in King of Prussia.

On the drive back to Philly Jimmy told Lisa about what him and her father talked about, Lisa was happy that her soon to be husband was building her hotel that she will be the Boss Lady of. Jimmy thinks to himself, things are going great between him and his soon to be wife. They have the house, cars, a family and in a couple of months they will be married Jimmy is thinking. "Lisa I love you so much and all I want is the best for you and our children, I gave the game up to spend the rest of my life with you and the kids. Now I know that I am going to have some problems with Nook taking my daughter from her but I have to do what is best for Narlyn and I think that you will be a better mother to her then Nook would be. I need to know if you're with me in this decision." "Baby

I will always have your back no matter what" Lisa says as she reaches over to give Jimmy a kiss on his cheek.

They get home and soon as they walked in the door Jimmy phone rings and it's Nook. "What does this girl want now?" He answers the phone and Nook is yelling, "YOU THINK YOU GOING TO TAKE MY DAUGHTER FROM ME!!!! Bring me my daughter home now Jimmy." "Nook received her court papers in the mail" says Jimmy to Lisa, court is on Monday and it's Jimmy's weekend to have his daughter. He has pictures and voice recordings that he has already given to his lawyer for court. The caseworker has already come out to look at Jimmy's house and where Narlyn was going to sleep. Also, the come caseworker went out to Nooks house that same day to make sure the child was living in a safe environment. "Nook I'm not bringing her home, this is my weekend with my daughter." "You going to send these people out to my house to see how I live Jimmy. You are not going to get my daughter" says Nook and "you act like you have a better place for her to stay Jimmy." Nook has never been to Jimmy's house, no one has ever been there except for his family, his boys and his fiancée that is living there now.

Monday arrived and Jimmy is getting ready for court. Lisa is going to stay home with the baby. Jimmy wants no drama with Nook and his fiancé. She doesn't need to be at court, the caseworker and lawyer already met Lisa they both love her and now it's time to take his daughter from Nook for good.

Jimmy calls Lisa and tells her the good news, "baby I have full custody of my daughter, Nook has to have visitation with her, but the caseworker will need to be present. Baby girl the judge put my daughter on her lap and asked her all kinds of questions, Narlyn said that she wanted to live with you and that took Nook over the roof when she said that. They pulled out all the pictures and played the recordings and baby you had to see Nooks face; she has to go to counseling to learn how to take care of a child. And guess what she is pregnant now and they are talking about taking that child from her too. She tried to say I sold drugs to get my car and that I live at home with my mother or whatever girl would allow me to live with them" Jimmy laughed. She was upset when she seen that I had a condo, she looked at the pictures of Narlyn room and tears started coming down her eyes. I made sure that she would never know where I live at. Your dad gave me an awesome recommendation letter to give to the courts to prove that I am working, plus I have pay stubs from my dad's company that goes back to when I was 17 years old. She just knew that she had something on me and it backfired on her, they were going to lock her up because of how she was acting, she tried to take Narlyn out of my hands as we were leaving the courtroom. My baby was screaming she didn't want to go with her mom."

Nook calls Jimmy's phone but he doesn't answer it, she left message after message on his phone telling him that he will get his, he's not keeping her daughter away from her. How the life that he is living with Lisa was supposed to be her life and his little girlfriend took it from her. Jimmy laughs at all the messages, Jimmy you will not make it to your wedding believe me when I tell you that and he heard a gunshot in the background. Now he didn't know if Nook shot herself or if she was telling him that she was going to kill him.

But what Nook didn't know that he had papers drawn up stating that if anything happens to him that his daughter Narlyn will live with Lisa for the rest of her life. Nook will never get her daughter back no matter what classes she goes to.

Jimmy stops at his mother's house so she can see her granddaughter, he hides his car five blocks away, Terri picked him up in her car. Jimmy was very smart he knew the tricks and trades the ins and outs, but Nook wasn't that smart she tried to find out where Jimmy was living. She stalked Lisa's mom's house, but she never saw Jimmy or Lisa come in or out of there.

Miss Kaye was Jimmy and Terri's mother, her and Miss Nae are twin sisters. Here's my grand baby says Miss Kaye as she gives Narlyn a big hug. Narlyn takes her grand mom cheeks and gives her a big kiss on the lips. Jimmy and Terri start laughing, that's her way of telling you that she likes you and that she's safe with you. I noticed that when she did it with Lisa. "She did the same thing to me" said Terri. "I been really paying close attention to how she reacts to things and people. If she doesn't feel safe with you she is going to cry and she will hide behind Lisa or myself." "Do you think that she was being abused?" asked Miss Kaye. "Mom anything is possible living with Nook, I know that she's not going to let her get molested because Nook was molested when she was a child, so I don't think that's the case. I just think Nook beat her and probably let her friends hit her if Nook wasn't around. Narlyn cries a lot so maybe they hit her thinking that it would make her stop crying. Each time I ask her did someone hit her before she gets quite so I'm taking it that someone has been beating on her. I talked with her and told her that she is safe now and that she doesn't have to worry about anyone ever hitting on her again. She is very smart at the age of three so if you ask her a question, she can answer it clearly and that you will understand what she is saying and talking about."

The visit was over with Jimmy's mother. "Terri, can you take me to my car?" Before they walked out the door Terri seen Nook standing on corner of Marshall & Green. She hurried up and pushed Jimmy back in the house.

"Terri what's up?", "Nook is out there on the corner by the bar talking to some guy. You go out the back door and meet at the end of the park on Chestnut Street side." At first Jimmy said he wasn't going to keep hiding from her but then he thought if she sees what kind of car, he was driving she was going to follow him all the way back to Philly. Now Jimmy had cousins and even his sister could fight Nook but he just wanted to stay as far away from her crazy butt as possible so he went out the back door and met his sister at the end of the park.

Terri dropped him off at his car, Terri gave her niece a kiss and hug. "Narlyn auntie will be down to see you this weekend." Narlyn smiled, "ok Tee Tee" she said. Jimmy closed the door and got into his car; Terri waited until he pulled off before pulling off herself.

When Terri got back to the house Nook walked up the street to where Terri was. "Terri, can I talk to you?" "Sure, what's up?" asked Terri. "Why is your brother doing this to me? He played me for one and then going to take my daughter from me like that's not cool and you know it's not Terri." "How did he play you Nook, y'all had what 1 or two nights with each other and you got pregnant and you decided to keep the baby. He didn't even know you was pregnant until you went into the hospital to have the baby, that's why he didn't think the baby was his because you never said anything to him about you being pregnant." "You think if I would have told him we would have been together?" Terri looked at Nook with a strange look, "Nook my brother never wanted to be in a relationship with anyone he always was a player until he saw Lisa." Terri knew she was making Nook mad by talking about Lisa. Nook couldn't stand Lisa the first day she saw her at the basketball courts that night in OD Park when they had the party there. Terri keep going on talking about how Jimmy is going to marry Lisa and how they are a family now and that she should just get over it so she can try and co parent with Jimmy. Nook wasn't trying to hear that she wanted Jimmy to suffer. "Well I just think he was wrong about me and he didn't really get the chance to find out what type of person I am." Terri chuckled a little bit before telling Nook she needs to move on with her life because Jimmy wasn't going to leave Lisa and his family for no one.

Terri called Jimmy and told him everything her and Nook talked about. "Jimmy, I don't know I just think really you need to get a restraining order on her seriously. The look that was in her eyes was like she wanted to kill you." "Listen I'm not worried about that girl she's just mad, I will stay away from her because I don't think she will try and hurt me as far as killing me or anything like that. I just think she will try to have me locked up so I can't get married and that she can try to take my daughter back from me. But I got things written on paper that she will never get Narlyn ever again I have full custody of my daughter and if anything happens to my wife will take over in my place." "Big brother just please watch her because I will be sitting behind bars if she does something to you so please be careful." "Ok I got you little sister I will hit you back later I just pulled up at the crib."

Jimmy told Lisa everything that was said, how him and his daughter had to sneak out the back door. Lisa laughed, "baby it's not funny she is crazy", Jimmy said "it is funny cause who acts like that over some sex for only two nights?' "You not only got one crazy chick you got two of them, the girl in New York what's her name Bianca girlfriend." Laughing Jimmy says "oh Tina yes I forgot about her I better stay clear of the both of them", Jimmy and Lisa laughed at the situation.

Lisa puts Narlyn and Jymayia down for the night, Jimmy is sitting out on the deck in their bedroom sipping on his favorite drink, Henny. "The stars are beautiful tonight" says Lisa as she lays in Jimmy's arms. "I spoke with your dad earlier today and he wants me to start on the hotel Monday." Jimmy wants to have the hotel done before the wedding. He wants to surprise Lisa by having the wedding at the church and then the reception at the hotel. That way if anyone had too much to drink they can get a room if they are too drunk to drive home. Lisa's father is going to have his crew help Jimmy out to get the job done in six months.

Terri is on her way to Philly to spend the weekend with Lisa, her brother and her nieces. She wanted to bring her boyfriend with her, but she knows Jimmy didn't want anyone to know where he lived.

"Baby can you get the door" says Lisa, Jimmy opens the door for his sister. "Big brother what's up?" Terri says as she walks in the house. "Jimmy, I love what you did with the house", Lisa comes out of the bedroom, "hey girl" she says to her best friend. "I was expecting you earlier I made dinner for us." "Well I wanted to bring Richard with me, but I knew that Jimmy didn't want anyone to know where he lives. So I spent some time with him before I came here." "That's fine girl I know how you feel, so where is my nieces at?" "Well Terri it is after 9 o'clock I put them down for bed already. We are out here sitting on the deck; you want a drink or something?" "Girl yes what y'all got?" "Girl you know I got your Vodka and Tonic already for you on ice", both of the ladies laughed like old times. Ever since Lisa started dating Jimmy her life has changed, and after she had Jymayia it changed even more. Lisa is a family woman now at the age of 19, all she wants is to be a good mother and wife to her family. The ladies stayed up half of the night talking, laughing and drinking. Jimmy had already gone to bed.

"Did Jimmy tell you about Nook? Lisa I am worried about my brother, this girl had this look in her eyes like she wanted to kill him or you. She just kept going on and on how she should have been his fiancé, the things he gave to you should have been hers. She was staring off into space as she was talking like she was picturing this big family that she had with my brother", laughs Terri. "Terri I am not worried about that girl or the other girl over in New York they fell in love with someone that they don't even know for one and for two he only had sex with the both of them two times and they are tripping like that. I'm not going to keep a baby by someone I don't know what he is about, Nook knows nothing about Jimmy." "Girl I know but she is on some if I can't have the family with him no one will." "Yeah he told me that he wants to try and stay away from Norristown as much as possible. Jimmy feels as though she will have him locked up for a long time or try to set him up to get robbed. He carries his gun with him every time he goes out of the house. He stopped selling drugs and he transferred most of his money into my account and his daughter's accounts. I believe he even put some into your moms account too. So he is aware of whatever she is trying to do, he's not scared or anything but he knows that a female will set a nigga up to get robbed and killed."

Saturday morning came and Lisa was up making breakfast for everyone. "Good morning baby girl" says Jimmy as he kissed Lisa. Terri walks into the kitchen rubbing her eyes, "sis how did you sleep last night?" asked Jimmy. "Not so well Jimmy, I been thinking about the conversation Nook and I had yesterday." "Terri listen I'm not going to say Nook is not capable of doing anything to me, but she has to understand there was never any feelings there and that she needs to get over it. I don't trust her or that crazy bat Tina but I'm not going to stop living my life because these chicks want something that they can't have."

The baby started crying. "I will be right back, let me go get Jymayia and wake Narlyn up so she can eat breakfast." Terri talks to her brother. She is very worried that Nook will try to do something to him. Jimmy you didn't see the look in that girl eyes, I saw nothing but blood in her eyes. I told her nothing better not happen to you or she will have to deal with a lot of people, and her stare was like she didn't care she had to get revenge on you. Jimmy just sat there for a second, "baby sister I hear everything that you are saying but I really don't think that she wants to hurt me in that way, I really thinks that she will try to get me locked up. She thinks that if I was to ever go to jail for a long time that she will get Narlyn back, and that I can't get married. That's one of the reasons why I come to Norristown see you and mom and roll back out without anyone knowing that I am in town." "Ok if you got this then I will leave it alone I'm not going to say nothing else about it."

Lisa walked back in the room with the girls, "TeeTee" says Narlyn as she ran to her aunt. Terri picks her niece up and gives her a hug and kiss, "you are getting heavy" as she tickles her. "Tee Tee that's my little sister over there and I love her TeeTee," "aww I love her too."

Jimmy phones rings and it's Nook. "Hey take her back in her room so she can play", "no Jimmy let her talk to her mom" says Lisa but put her on speaker phone. Jimmy answered the phone, "hello" says Jimmy. "Jimmy where is my daughter?", "she is right here", "can I talk to her?", "yes your sure can, come here baby talk to your mom." Narlyn didn't move she just looked at her dad. "Narlyn come talk to your mom," Narlyn got up and walked to her dad. She spoke very low and said "hi mom". "GIRL WHAT ARE YOU WHISPERING FOR!!!" said Nook yelling at her, Narlyn jumped a little bit before she answered. "Hi mom" she said a little louder, "how you doing? How are they treating you?" "Mom they are treating me good, Lisa gives me baths and reads me bedtime stories." Nook got quiet, "put your dad on the phone." "Hello, Jimmy why is this little girl acting like she is her mother." "Nook while my daughter is here with my fiancée she is going to take care of her the way she needs to be taken care of." "What are you trying to say I'm not a good mother cause your wrong, you come to court with all that stuff and have them take my daughter from me so you and your little girlfriend can play house with her and your other ugly baby." Lisa wants to say something, but Jimmy stopped her. "Nook I told you before to stop calling my baby names, you need to grow up, my Jymayia did nothing wrong to you." "Oh so you gave her part of your name" laughs Nook. "Tee Tee can you walk me to my room" says Narlyn with a sad voice. "Listen I got to go if you don't want nothing else your daughter will talk to you later." "Jimmy, I want to see my daughter" "you will see her when you are setup with a caseworker, until then you will not hurt, scare or yell at her ever again" and Jimmy hung the phone up.

Jimmy was mad and Lisa is trying everything she can to calm him down. "Lisa did you see how my daughter jumped when she started yelling at her, and she thinks I'm going to let her see her! No I don't care what she is thinking in her head of doing to me I will make sure my daughter never goes back to her!", he yells. "My daughter is very scared of her own mother Lisa." "Jimmy, I know but you are yelling that isn't making it any better." "Narlyn come her baby", says Jimmy. She comes and jumps up in his lap. "Baby you don't ever in your life have to be scared of your mother, I will never let her hurt you ever again" he said as he shed a tear from his eye. Jimmy hugged her so tight, "daddy will never hurt you either I love you baby." Narlyn said "I love you too daddy, I love Lisa and TeeTee too daddy", "and they love you too" said Jimmy as he smiled at his daughter.

98

Jimmy got dressed to head out to New York to see his boys. Lisa took the girls and Terri to see Terri's Aunt Nae. On their way to North Philly Terri's cousin Mimi called her, "hey cuz what's up, hey who this girl Nook?" "What? How do you know about her?" asked Terri? "She called my phone asking all these questions like she was the police, I told her to get off my line with that mess. I asked her how she got my number and she said don't worry about it just know that all of Jimmy's family is going to get theirs one by one." "Oh Jimmy lost his phone that day we were at her house and she tried to tell him he didn't leave it there. He got a new phone but with the same number." "Where is my cousin at because girlfriend barking up the wrong tree, I will give her what she is asking for." "Oh, wow he lost his phone like two weeks ago, right before they went to court, matter of fact he left it at the court house and when he went back to look for it he couldn't find it". Laughing Terri says, "I can't wait to tell Jimmy she took his phone, Mimi she is crazy in love with Jimmy." "Well she is going to be crazy in love with my fist in her eyes if she keeps calling my phone, she has been calling and hanging up on me for a week now, this is the first time that she said something. Is that Narlyn's mother?" "Yes Mimi, we talked yesterday, and she was talking like she wanted to do something to my brother." "Do something like what?" "I don't know but when she was talking her eyes looked like she wanted to kill him, she was looking off into space somewhere as she was talking. I told Jimmy and he seems to think that she would have him locked up so he won't be home for him and Lisa's wedding." "He has a sister and plenty of girl cousins why he didn't say something about this girl." "Mimi I really can't say right now but we about to pull up to your house and we can talk about it then", "ok see you soon."

Once Terri and Lisa got to Aunt Nae's house Terri called Jimmy and told him everything that Mimi said to her. She probably called everyone in his contacts. "That's strange" said Jimmy "because she hasn't called Lisa's phone yet." "Right Jimmy, Mimi said that she would call and hang up but this time she said that everyone needs to watch their backs." "Terri I'm not really worried about her, we talked about this already let it go she not going to do anything to anyone. Her problem is with me not no one else not even Lisa so I wouldn't worry about her. I'm about to get married in a couple of months Nook is the last person and thing that is on my mind right now."

Monday came and it's Jimmy's first day at the construction site. He worked from 5am until 7pm that night. Jimmy is trying to make sure that the hotel is done by the time of the wedding so that they can have the reception there. He wants this to be special for Lisa, the love of his life. He is not going to let anything, or anybody stand in his way of marrying Lisa, he loves her until "death do them part."

Months went on with Jimmy working day and night to get the hotel ready for the wedding. He would call Lisa and the girls and talk to them while he was working to make sure that there're ok. Lisa told Jimmy that she was getting strange phone calls from a blocked number. She knew it was Nook playing on her phone, but Lisa didn't play games like that and she wants to confront her. "Lisa please not right now, after we get married and if you, Terri and Mimi want to go to her house then that's fine with me but right now whatever Nook has up her sleeves with me I will handle it. Right now, we need to just let it go, I will talk with the caseworker and see if we can get a restraining order on her for right now."

Lisa is not the one to play with, she thinks to herself once she gets her hands on that girl, she is going to tear her out the frame. "Lisa, I don't want my daughter to see or hear us doing anything to her mother, so I rather let the courts handle this." "Ok but if she keeps playing on my phone Jimmy, I might not wait for the courts to handle it because I'm going to handle it" as she hangs up on him. This is exactly what Nook wanted for Jimmy and Lisa to go at each other thinking that it will get so bad that Lisa will leave him, and he will come to her.

CHAPTER EIGHT

immy and his crew are now three months into the project of building
the hotel. He has three more months to go before the wedding. He
has a court date coming up where he has to face Nook again, he
hasn't seen her in four months. Each time it was time for her to see Narlyn
the caseworker will come get her and take her to the appointment to see
her mother. Nook has been calling Jimmy and Lisa's phones playing on
them. It got so bad that Jimmy wanted to change his number, but he knows
that he will have to contact each person and let them know that his number
has been changed, and he doesn't want to do that. On the other hand, Lisa
just doesn't answer her phone if the number is not stored in her phone
under a name, she will not answer it. But see Nook is so petty that she
leaves messages saying stuff like tell your fiancé to stop calling me all times
of the night, or why your man asking me for pictures of me things like that.

Jimmy and Lisa have been arguing with each other behind Jimmy not
saying anything to Nook about what she is doing and saying. Now Lisa is
starting to think is he cheating on me with her, is her saying these things
to her true. All Jimmy is trying to do is protect his daughter from all the
nonsense that her mother is causing between him and Lisa.

Jimmy comes home from work early this one night, he's usually there by 8:30 at night but this time he left work at 5pm so he can spend some time with Lisa. Dinner was cooked and the girls were fed, Lisa was in the bathroom giving Narlyn a bath. Jimmy walked in the bathroom, he reached down to give Lisa a kiss but Lisa turned her head. "Baby we need to talk" says Jimmy, "I'm not feeling this vibe between you and I" he says. "Ok after I finish giving the girls their baths" as a tear rolls down Lisa eye. She put both girls in Narlyn's room to watch TV, Jymayia was now five months so she loved to watch cartoons with her sister. Lisa walked into the living room where Jimmy was sitting looking out the window. "What's up" says Lisa? "Baby girl listen I know it's been a rough five months but I figure if I kept you away from the drama everything would have been fine." "Ok so what do you mean away from the drama, is there something going on between you and her, was you sending her pictures of you, and was you asking her for pictures of her." "Lisa sit down I mean this from my heart, I will never cheat on you, I love you and I want to spend the rest of my life with you. I don't want Nook or any other female for that matter. I made a mistake by even getting that girl pregnant, but it all happened before you and I started dealing with each other Lisa, so I don't understand why we are even going through what we are going through."

"Jimmy this girl has threatened you, been calling your family and has been calling my phone and the only thing you have been saying is "don't worry about her" what does that mean Jimmy?" "Lisa I can't stop her from doing what she is doing, I pay her no mind she just wants to try and break us up and to stop the wedding which is not going to happen. I'm going to marry you regardless and I'm going to have a happy family Lisa, she is not going to stop this." Tears are rolling down Lisa's eyes, Jimmy pulls her close to him he starts kissing on her lips then her neck she feels his erection and stops him. "Jimmy the kids are woke in the other room." Jimmy gets up to check on the kids and they are laying down into the TV, "Narlyn is everything ok?" he asked his daughter to make sure there will be no interruptions. "Yes, daddy we are just watching cartoons."

Jimmy goes back out into the living room lays Lisa down in front of the fireplace and makes passionate love to her. "Baby girl when I told you I have your back I got your back; I will never let anyone hurt you." Lisa shakes her head and says "ok" before she tells him that she loves him.

They end up falling asleep in the living room. It was 12 midnight when Jimmy's phone rings. He looks at the number and it was Nook. He didn't answer the phone, he turned the phone off and went in and checked on the kids to make sure they were tucked in and asleep. He went back into the living room and cuddled under Lisa.

The next morning came Jimmy got up around 4am and got ready for work. He turned his phone on and he saw that he had 31 message on his phone and they all was from Nook. He saw one was from his cousin Mimi, it read cousin listen this girl is really asking for it call me once you get this text. Jimmy didn't call Mimi. Jimmy didn't want to deal with this he is upset with his self for even dealing with this crazy girl. So while he was in the car on his way to work he called Nook. "Hello" she answered, "Nook what is wrong with you, my family has nothing to do with you or me. Why do you keep calling my cousin Mimi? Why did you keep my phone? I don't know what you're trying to do but sweetie it's not going to work. My fiancé and I are still going to get married; we still will have a family and Narlyn is going to be a part of the family Nook so just leave us alone." "Well, why did he say that", Nook started yelling in the phone calling Jimmy all kinds of names, telling him she was going to hurt him bad. Jimmy hung the phone up on her, laughed and turned his music up as he drove down the highway to King of Prussia.

Within the three months of Jimmy and the crew working day in and day out they have all of the outside of the hotel done, now they are working to get the inside done. The hotel will have a large ball room, swimming pool, tennis court, game room, casino, and go carts he is also making a three-bedroom three-bathroom loft with a nice size kitchen for Lisa when they want to get away. The hotel will be eight stories high with 800 rooms, each room will have a TV, living room area, bathroom, fireplace, balcony, one or two beds and a small size kitchen.

It's 8pm and Jimmy is done for the night. He heads home so he can spend time with Lisa and his two daughters. "Hello" says Lisa, "hey baby girl what are you doing?" asked Jimmy. "I just got finished giving the girls a bath and putting them to bed, and I was waiting for my man to come home." "I'm on my way to you right now baby girl I love you and see you soon", "ok" says Lisa as she hangs up the phone.

Jimmy pulls up to the house and his neighbor is standing outside drunk. He pulls the car into the garage. "Hey Mr. Watson" he says as he walks over to him, "hey Jimmy can you help me into my house?" Jimmy helps him into his house before going into his house, Lisa is sitting on the sofa waiting for him. "Hey baby girl daddy's home" laughs Jimmy, he sits down beside her, she had her head down, "hey baby girl what's the matter?" "Jimmy this girl has to stop playing on my phone, I told you before I may be young, but I don't play the kids games with no one. This girl got what four years over me and she is playing kid games like this. She called I answered the phone and she start off is this Lisa, so I say yes this is her. She goes on to say just to let you know Jimmy been asking me can he come to my house, so I played her game and asked her when he asked her that. She says he just called me not to long ago he said he was at his mom house and he is on his way to my house. I knew she was lying because I just got off the phone with you and you said that you will be here in 10 mins. I said oh ok so when he gets there tell him to call home, she laughs and says no he not coming home and hung up the phone. "Look this is her calling again", Lisa answers the phone you hear moaning on the phone "you're a sick girl you need to go get you some help" says Lisa before hanging up the phone. Jimmy calls Nook he puts her on speaker, "hello" answers Nook laughing 'hey my love "she says "what are you doing calling me, what your girl going to say about this?" "My girl is not going to say anything because I'm sitting here with her right now." Click is all you hear on the other end. "See baby girl she just wants us to argue she doesn't want us to be happy Lisa and your falling right into what she is doing."

Two weeks went by and they have not got any calls from Nook. Jimmy is almost finished with the hotel project just in time for the wedding which will be in a month in a half.

Jimmy is done for the night and he is heading home from work, he calls Lisa to check on her and the girls, "baby girl I will be there soon love you and see you soon."

"Jimmy. I want to go to Norristown to see my sisters, I haven't seen them in over three months Jimmy. Jymayia is six months now and I want her to spend time with her aunts." Jimmy looks at Lisa in fear that her and Nook will cross paths with one and another, he doesn't want Lisa to get into it with Nook. "Ok I will take you to town this weekend coming", "Jimmy I can drive myself that's why you got me a car right?" she asks. "Lisa listen I know you want to see your family but", "but what Jimmy?

I'm not scared nor am I going to hide from no one. Besides she doesn't know what kind of car I will be driving."

Saturday morning Lisa gets Jymayia and Narlyn dressed and ready to go to Norristown and spend time with her sisters. Now she knows that someone is going to tell Nook that her daughter was in town but Lisa is ready for whatever. Nook has been talking about Jymayia calling her names and playing on Lisa's phone, so Lisa is ready for mess if Nook wants to bring it.

Lisa calls Terri and tells her that she is on her way to Norristown to visit her sisters and that she will stop pass there to see her while she is in town.

Lisa arrives to Norristown, she pulls up in front of her mom's house, she gets out of the car feeling strange cause she knows that her mother will not be in the house. Lisa has not been to the house since her and her sisters cleaned the house out with her mother things and gave them to Goodwill. She takes Jymayia out the car first, then Narlyn, "Lisa!!!" screams her sister Linda as she runs to her and gives her a hug. She takes the baby out of Lisa's hand, "hey little one "she says to her niece "I haven't seen you in three months."

Terri walks up the street to see her nieces and best friend. Narlyn runs "Tee Tee" she says as she jumps into her arms. "Hey baby" she gives her niece a kiss before putting her down, "you want to go see grandma?" she asks. Narlyn shakes her head yes so Terri says, "I will be right back let me take Narlyn to see my mom." Jimmy calls Terri, "hey did you take Narlyn to mommy's house, yeah she is going to stay there until Lisa is ready to leave, she still has to bring the baby down to see mommy."

Terri, Lisa and her sisters are sitting outside of her mother's house and a car pulls up. Lisa turns and looks and its Nook with two other girls in the car. Their eyes meet and you can just see the steam in Nook's eyes once she realizes that it's Lisa. She circles around the block and pulls right up in front of Lisa's mother house. "Little girl do you have my daughter with you?", Lisa just looked at her, she put Jymayia in her car seat walked over to the car but before she can even do anything Nook pulled out some mace and tried to mace Lisa. But Lisa stepped back just in time. She runs up to the car but before she can swing at Nook she pulled off. Lisa is upset now she is pacing back and forth talking to herself. I'm a kill this girl she said I'm a kill her. Linda came to the door, "Lisa what's a matter with you?" "Linda this girl just came here while I have my daughter out here and tried to mace me I am going to kill her Linda I mean that on my mother I am going to kill her." "What girl Lisa? Who came pass here?" "Narlyn mother Linda I'm a kill her" Lisa starts crying. She calls Jimmy screaming in the phone "I AM GOING TO KILL YOUR BABY MOM!!!!!" and she hung the phone up. Nook calls Lisa's phone laughing, "pull up" Lisa said, "put you mace down and pull up." Nook kept laughing so that made Lisa angrier she told her sister to watch Jymayia she was going to Nooks house. Linda grabbed her, "you are not going anywhere if that girl really wanted to fight, she would have got out of the car Lisa." "Linda, she tried to mace me when my daughter was right there", Linda sat Lisa down "listen she is not worth you going to jail Lisa. She didn't hit you or your daughter with the mace so chill out, if she comes back around then I'm a let you handle your business she will need to get out of the car."

Nook comes back around the block again and this time Terri, Linda, Laura and Lisa are outside. Nook slows down as she was driving, "get out the car and fight my sister" says Linda, Nook laughs and next thing you know Lisa threw a brick at her and it hit the back window and shattered almost made Nook crash.

She pulls the car over and jumps out Lisa runs down the street and they start fighting. One of Nooks friends get out the car like she was going to jump in it and Terri pushed her. I wish you would try to jump my best friend. Linda and Laura are there to make sure no one else tries to jump in the fight. Lisa has Nook on the ground kicking her in the face. Nook curls up in a ball, but Lisa kept kicking and kicking. Laura pulls Lisa away and when Nook got up, she was in a daze almost fell back to the ground. Lisa was still trying to get to her, but her sisters were pulling her back telling her to chill.

"If you ever try to come for me again girl, I will hurt you bad" said Lisa as she spits in Nooks face. She looked at Tiffany, "do you want what your girl just got?" as she stepped back in the street telling Tiffany to come in the street. Laura grabs Lisa and took her in the house to calm her down. Lisa was very mad at this point and really no one could ever clam Lisa down but her mother and she's not there so her sisters tried to do the best that they could to calm her down.

Jymayia started crying and that snapped Lisa back in place, "hey little mama I am sorry" she says as she held her daughter close to her with tears rolling down her eyes. Jimmy called Lisa's phone numerous of times, but she didn't answer, he called Terri's phone finally. "Terri where is Lisa?" he yelled in the phone, "she is right here"," put her on the phone." "Lisa this is why I didn't want you to go to Norristown I knew this was going to happen and you got the kids with you too." Lisa really wasn't listening to what Jimmy was saying all she wanted to do was hold her daughter.

The police pulled up, and Nook also pulled up behind the police. Linda went out to talk to them, "is that the cops" asked Jimmy? "Yes, Jimmy" she said with a stern voice. "I will call you back and let you know what happened click." Lisa is boiling right now she wants to hurt Nook bad. She walks outside and Nook tries to run up on her. The female officer grabs her and slams her on the car, she puts Nook in handcuffs and sits her in the patrol car. Lisa explains everything to the police, from the court date to today with the fight. Lisa is willing to pay for the window she says that's not a problem, but she is not going to keep harassing me because I'm not sure what will happens next officer. I don't bother anybody, and this girl keeps bothering me because I am engaged to a man that she slept with two times.

They took Nook out of the car told her that she is to stay away from Lisa and that they both will have a court date coming up, because Nook pressed charges Lisa did the same thing so she wouldn't get into serious trouble cause what she did to Nook's face.

Lisa goes to see Jimmy's mother before heading back to Philly, Jimmy was in New York so even if he wanted to come home, he wouldn't make to his fiancée in time. "Hello" said Lisa, "baby girl listen I am sorry for yelling at you, but I knew Nook was going to run into you. She hangs over that way cause Tiffany family lives on Marshall Street." "Jimmy it's all good I don't run from no one she will think again before she runs up on me again." "Lisa listen that girl is crazy" said Terri, and Jimmy said the same thing through the phone. "Ok she is not that crazy because I will hurt that lady badly, she doesn't know me at all and for that matter y'all really don't know me. I'm quiet but I also don't play any games with male or female I will fight trust me. What time are you leaving to go back home?" asked Jimmy. "I'm about to leave now, Terri is coming back with me." "Alright drive safe and I will see you when I come home. Lisa I love you. Nook is the last person you have to worry about, I don't want her and never will want her." "Jimmy I'm not worried at all if you do want her or not I'm just not going to be out here fighting over no man."

They get back to Philly and Lisa receives a call from Nook but Lisa didn't answer the call, she is fed up with Nook and her mess. "Terri can you believe this, why is this girl keep calling my phone like me beating you up and almost bashing your head into the ground is not good enough for her" laughs Lisa.

They pull up to the house and Jimmy is home waiting to see his three favorite girls. She opens the door and Narlyn runs and jumps into her dad's arms. "Hey sweetie you have fun today with grand mom", Narlyn shook her head and told her dad that she wanted to spend the weekend with her grand mom. Jimmy looks at his daughter at this point not sure on what to say, "sure baby one weekend you can go spend the weekend with grand mom and Tee Tee, now go in your room and watch TV so Lisa and I can talk." "Lisa do you want to tell me what happen between you and Nook?" "Jimmy listen this girl thinks that she is going to scare me away from Norristown she is sadly mistaken. I'm sitting outside with my sisters and she rides down the street, she sees me sitting out there I guess so she keeps riding. Mind you she was by herself, so I guess she went and got her friends and came back like I was supposed to be scared of them. She pulls up in front of my mother's house and asks me is her daughter up here but she calls me a little girl. I go to walk up to the car, and she pulls out this mace and tries to mace me, but I step back in time. Jimmy if that would have got on Jymayia I would have been in jail right now cause to me it looks like she was aiming for my daughter. She pulled off laughing then had the nerve to come back around the block like I was sweet like that Jimmy. She spits at me and I threw a brick at her car and she almost crashed, she jumps out the car like she was about to do something, so I ran up on her and it was over from there Jimmy. This woman is not going to intimidate me because she thinks I'm some little girl Jimmy. Then her girlfriend tried to run up on the fight and Terri pushed her out the way. My sisters are too old to get into my fights but they are not going to let no one jump me. I knew once I go to Norristown that I was going to run into that girl, but she's not going to keep me from going to see my sisters or even taking Jymaiya to see her grandmother. If she wants to fight every time I come to town then that is what is going to happen. I respect Narlyn but her mother doesn't respect her at all Jimmy."

"Lisa I am sorry that you have to deal with this, all I was trying to do was to keep you from getting in trouble with the law. I was keeping you from your family and my mother just so you and Nook wouldn't run into each other." "Jimmy I am going to run into this woman one day with you or by myself, she is not going to put fear in me Jimmy cause I'm younger than her. She's a little crazy but Jimmy I can take care of myself when it comes to someone disrespecting me." "Ok" says Jimmy "I will leave it alone, but I don't want you going to town without me for a while", "that's fine Jimmy" says Lisa.

CHAPTER NINE

The hotel is finally finished, and the wedding is two weeks away. Jimmy is having his bachelor's party tonight and Lisa is having her bachelorette party tonight as well. The men are at Raheem's house in New York, Bianca and the kids are at the house but out of the way of the party. Tina knows that Jimmy is having his bachelor party there at Raheem's house so she decides to show up later on that night when she thought that Jimmy was good and drunk. She knocks on the door around 1am in the morning, Raheem answers the door. "Hey, Raheem is B still up?" He invites her in because the last he saw Bianca she was getting the baby a bottle for bed.

" B" he yelled up the steps, "yes" she answered, "Tina is down here for you." Bianca looks at the time and wonders to herself why is Tina there this time of night and the same time that Jimmy is having his bachelor party. "Ok I will be down in a minute tell her."

Tina creeps into the other room where the guys are at, peeking through the door she spots Jimmy. Boy he looks so good she thinks to herself, "hey girl" says Bianca as she startled Tina. "Oh hey B, what's up?" "You Tina" says Bianca, "what brings you here this time of night" as if she doesn't know the answer to the question. "It's a Friday night I wanted to know if you wanted to go out with me", Bianca laughed Tina it is 1 o'clock in the morning "it's a party going on in the other room why will I be going out with no one to babysit my children Tina.?" "What is really going on she asked". "B, I need to talk to you please." "Ok come on upstairs and we can talk while I'm putting the baby to bed." Tina follows Bianca upstairs to the baby's room, "B I can't get him off of my mind", "who is you talking about?" asked Bianca. "Jimmy" she says as she gets up and walks to the window and looks out of it. "This man made good love to me B and I can't get that off of my mind. Yes, he was drunk but the way he kissed my body and the things he did to me is what turned me on. It's like I want that sexual feeling from him again and again." "Tina you do know that this man is about to get married to the love of his life next week?" "Yes, B, I do know that but if I can just have one more night with him I can make him leave her" she says. Laughing Bianca says :wait you actually think Jimmy is going to leave Lisa for you, Tina that's not going to happen he loves that girl that's all he talks about is her. He sung this song in front of all of us earlier of what he was going to sing to her as she is walking down the aisle Tina, sweetie you, his other baby mama or anyone else for that matter is not going to take that man away from her."   "B we will see about that", Tina said as she stormed out of the room and down the steps slamming the door behind her. Tina sits in her car crying, thinking how she can take Jimmy away from Lisa.

"Baby what is going on?" asked Raheem, "Rah, Tina came here thinking that she can sleep with Jimmy for one more night before he gets married. Raheem it was wired on how she was saying he made love to her the first time they did it. She told me he was drunk, but the sex was very different than anyone else's that she has ever been with. She wants to take him away from Lisa." Raheem laughs, "yeah I want to see that happen because that man is very much in love with Lisa and all he keeps talking about is how beautiful she is going to look walking down the aisle."

"Tina needs to get it through her head that it was only one or two nights that they had sex, when she knocked on the door tonight, I thought to myself why this girl is here. To be honest with you I thought she was going to ask can she talk to Jimmy, but she asked for you." "Raheem, I know what Tina is about and I am worried that she might do something if not tonight maybe the day of the wedding. Talk to Jimmy and just tell him to be careful around her that he is never alone with her. "

So the party went on until the next morning, the men finally wind down and took it down and went to sleep. Tina was still sitting outside of Bianca and Raheem's house waiting for Jimmy to leave. Bianca saw that her car was still out there. She walks out to her car and taps on the window. "Hey girl what are you doing Tina sitting out here all night like this?" "B, I was drinking so I didn't want to drive home drunk." "Girl go home and sleep it off and we will talk later" said Bianca. It's time, the day has come of the wedding and Lisa, her two sisters and Terri are getting ready for the wedding. Terri is the matron of honor and Lisa's two sisters are one of the bridesmaids, Mimi and Kayla are also bridesmaids. Lisa's girlfriend from Chester is also in the wedding.

Jimmy's men, his best man is Raheem, groomsmen are Kyle, Brick, Marcus, Raymond and Raheem's little brother. Narlyn is the flower girl and Raheem's son is the ring boy. The wedding is about to begin, Jimmy is singing Lady I love you by O'Bryan as Lisa's father walks her down the aisle. You hear the whispers, she looks beautiful, Jimmy almost dropped the mic when he seen his wife to be, his eyes lit up and a smile came across his face but he had to pull it together to finish his song to her. When she got close he sang louder "LISA GIVE ME YOUR HAND SAY THAT I CAN BE YOUR MAN AND I WILL NEVER LET YOU DOWN YOU ASK ME IF I LOVE YOU ALL I DO IS SAY OHHH LISA I LOVE YOU." Tears were in Jimmy's eyes as he finished his song to her. He stared her in her eyes and said" I love you Lisa I need you more than sun light." She wiped his tears, the preacher asked for the rings they both said their vows. When it was time to say I do Jimmy kissed his new wife like he was making love to her, everyone was crying including the groomsmen.

Everyone was at the reception waiting for Jimmy and Lisa to get there. Jimmy carried her into the hall of the new hotel he built with Lisa's eyes closed. Lisa didn't even know that the hotel was done. He put her down and said with the sexiest voice in her ear open your eyes. The ball room was done up in all her favorite colors with streamers, balloons, plenty of food and desserts were lined up nice and neat across five tables. The cake was huge with two dolls on top looked just like Jimmy and Lisa. She cried, he hugged her and took his thumb and wiped her tears then he kissed them.

The party went on and now it was time for the bride and groom to dance together. The song "You & I" by Jodeci came on and Jimmy pulled Lisa close to him as he sings in her ear. She felt his erection, but she didn't say anything she just kept dancing. Jimmy was so far going with everything he didn't care all he wanted was to hold her and didn't care if there were people in the room or not. He thought to his self I waited too long for this day to come and I am going to enjoy every moment of it. After the song was over Lisa pulled his shirt out of his pants so no one would see what was going on. The reception went on for six hours and all the rooms were free for those who wanted to stay. Jimmy took his wife and kids to their loft which Lisa hasn't seen yet. "Jimmy you just did your thing with this hotel I love every bit of it", says Lisa.

Two days after the wedding Jimmy and Lisa was supposed to go on their honeymoon, they were going to the Bahamas for a week but that didn't happen. Jimmy left the house around 8 o'clock in the morning for the last court date he has with Nook. Time went by and it was now 4pm. Lisa called Jimmy's phone and it kept going to voicemail. Lisa didn't think anything about it because she knows that court can take most of the day. It's now 6:30 in the evening and Jimmy still hasn't come home. Now all kinds of thought are going through Lisa's mind. She called Terri and asked if she seen him and Terri said No he never came there or called to let anyone know he was coming to town for court. She calls Kyle, Raheem and Brick and neither one of them seen him. It's now 9 o'clock and Lisa is ready to take Jimmy's head off his shoulders when he walks through that door she doesn't want to hear no excuses.

Lisa is sitting in the living room drinking a glass of wine and it is now 11:15 pm and Lisa is now heated. As she goes to pick the phone up to call him the 10th time his phone is still going to voicemail. The doorbell rings, Lisa thinks to herself who could this be this time of night, no one knows where Jimmy lives. She peeks out the peep hole and it is two men in suits. "Hi, can I help you?" Lisa says not wanting to open the door. "Hi is this Jimmy Smith's house?" one of the men said," yes" answered Lisa "how can I help you?" "My name is Detective Warner, this is my partner Detective Gross and we are with the Philadelphia Homicide Department may we please talk to you?" Now Lisa is thinking what Jimmy did two days after they got married. Did he kill Nook she thought to herself? Ok she opens the door and one of the men say, "Are you Mrs. Smith?", "yes what's going on?" "Mrs. Smith I really don't know how to tell you this, but we found", before the Detective can get it out of his mouth Lisa says "what is going on? Where is my husband? We just got married two days ago." "I'm sorry but your husband's body was found in his car in Norristown, they called our Homicide department to come here." Lisa screams "NOOOOO!!!" it woke the kids up and her neighbor up too by her scream. Her neighbor runs over to see if everything was ok with Lisa, the older lady grabs Lisa and asks what's going on. "Jimmy was killed", she screamed crying. She sat Lisa down on the sofa so the detectives can talk with her. "Mrs. Smith, do you know why Jimmy was in Norristown today?", "Yes he had court with his daughter's mother at 11 o'clock this morning." "Well he never made it to court, his body was in his car since 9:30 this morning on the 500 block of Dekalb Street." "That's around the corner from his mother's house" she says, "ok do you think he was going to see his mother before court started." "I don't know", cried Lisa "I have to call his mother please excuse me." Terri, please answer the phone, "hello" Terri answered. "Lisa what's the matter?" she asked not knowing what is going on. "Terri my husband is dead!" she cried falling to her knees.

"Mom-Mom!!!!" Terri screams, "Terri why are you screaming my name like that?" "Mom this is Lisa on the phone there are detectives at her house, and they said that they found Jimmy in his car dead here in Norristown on the 500 block of Dekalb Street." Kaye puts on her clothes, her and Terri runs around the corner on Dekalb Street and they see that it was all taped off and it was a lot of people out there.

Jimmy's mom grabs Terri and they're both crying. Lisa calls Kyle and tells him what happened, "Yo, I'm on my way to pick you up. Kayla will watch the kids while we go to Norristown." Kyle calls Raheem and Brick and they are on their way to Norristown. Kyle is doing 100 on the highway.

Mimi is holding Lisa, Marcus is crying staring out the window, Ms. Nae is shaking crying saying not my nephew.

Everyone gets to Norristown; they are all at Jimmy's mom's house. Lisa's sisters are there too. It was quiet and all you hear is Lisa scream "WHY!!!! Jimmy why" as she broke down to the ground. Her sisters were kneeled down beside her, "Linda he was supposed to be here to take care of us I am pregnant again and I wanted to surprise him when he got home. If I find this girl had something to do with my husband getting killed Linda, I'm going to kill her I mean that on everything I love."

A week has passed by and it was time for Jimmy's funeral service. Everyone was stunned that Jimmy was gone. Lisa, Kyle, Raheem and Terri knew it had to be either Nook or Tina who had something to do with Jimmy's murder.

AUTHOR'S BIO

Victoria Hall, born and raised in Norristown Pennsylvania, is a supervisor at Phoenixville Hospital in the Dietary Department and an author of "My Best Friend's Brother". She had written the same book many years back when she was only 16 but didn't have the chance to proceed with it because she wanted to gain more experience from life. Finally, at the age of 53, she accomplished one of her goals to be a tremendous writer. However, it was really difficult to still remember all the thoughts after so many years.

Besides writing, she also enjoys reading drama, romance, fiction, and non-fiction books and novels as well. A deep thinker who likes to interact with people and sometimes makes herself busy playing popular video games to ease her mind from stress. Victoria is an honest God-fearing woman who also likes to read the Bible and listen to the word of God. She is thankful to God for giving her the opportunity and strength to write this book.

CPSIA information can be obtained
at www.ICGtesting.com
Printed in the USA
BVHW062301250221
601130BV00002B/296